THE PROMISED LAND DIARIES

2

The Laughing Princess of the Desert

The Diary of Sarah's Traveling Companion

Diary One
Sarai the Princess

2091 B.C.–2090 B.C.

Household Tree

We live on the go, but here are the people most important to me in our "household" . . .

Me, Rhoda: I'm seven years old.
Javen: My big brother is fifteen years old.
Dibri: Our baby brother is four, almost five, and into everything.
Abram: The head of everything and is very old—seventy-five!
Sarai: Though not as old as her husband, Abram, Sarai's old too—sixty-five.
Pigat: Ny new friend is eleven.
Gamilat: Another new friend is twelve.

At Haran, My Home

It's the cool of the day, and even from inside my tent on my bed mat I can feel that the sun has nearly set and released most of its heat. A soft breeze billows the tent walls. This is my favorite time. Our tent is made of goat hair, so there are tiny spaces between the woven threads, and through these spaces I see the sun setting from a sky that stretches above like a canopy. I can lie on my back and gaze at the thinly veiled heavens above. There's a full moon tonight and not a wisp of a cloud. Soon the purple sky will darken and a million stars will blink at me.

I hear the gentle "baas" and "bleats" of the sheep and goats as they settle into their fold for the evening. There is always the danger that lions and bears will attack the flocks, so the boys from the camp, including my big brother, watch them in shifts. I'm seven, but my brother Javen, who's fifteen, says I'm very grown-up and outspoken for my age. Our little brother, Dibri, is only four, in many ways still a baby. This is the first time I have ever written on my own parchment. Javen gave it to me on my birthday last week. He made it himself from the skin of a goat. The hammered hide is very smooth, but sometimes when I write, my pen stumbles across a tiny black hair that was never plucked from the skin! I have to use Javen's inkpot and reed pen until I can get my own, but he's a giving big brother . . . sometimes, at least.

Most girls are not taught to write. We learn to cook and spin and clean and take care of children. The boys are taught their fathers' crafts. If they learn to write, it's because they'll need this skill when they're grown men. They may have to write a contract between themselves and their neighbors. They may have to sign their names to legal transactions. Girls aren't allowed to handle such matters, so writing is considered a waste of time.

Not for me. I'm lucky because Javen didn't think it would be a waste of time to write. He taught me how. Actually, I pestered him to teach me until he gave in and said I drove him to teach me! Even though he complains, he does it with a smile. I don't think he minds so much, and he seems very proud of me. He reminds me that I'm the only girl, and the youngest person, he's ever known who writes. Most of the time he's a very good brother . . .

He has to be. Mama died four years ago as she gave birth to Dibri. Then Papa died just last year from the fever. He was a shepherd and a good friend to Abram. Abram is our neighbor . . . only now he's more. He's our family, I guess. After Papa died, Abram and Sarai were kind enough to take us in and look after us. They feed us, and we live with them.

Javen didn't want to go at first. He said he was old enough to be a man, and he wanted to take care of us by himself. That changed the day after we buried Papa in the cave. Abram came by our house. He took Javen outside, and they sat on some rocks and talked. I couldn't stand not knowing what Abram came to talk over with Javen, so I crouched down by the window and tried to listen.

Abram said, "I could use another shepherd. You're very good, Javen, just like your father. The good Lord knows that Sarai needs help around the camp. Rhoda would be a great asset to her. We'll leave Haran soon and head south into Canaan. Will you join our household?"

Abram is very smart. He knew that Javen would want to take care of our family on his own. Javen felt so responsible, and he promised Papa he would do this. But Abram knew Javen wasn't completely a grown-up yet. It'd be hard for even the most experienced parent to keep track of me and Dibri. Even I knew that. Papa had a difficult time keeping us in order and providing our meals. He got so tired that I think that's what made him get sick. Abram also knew we had sold most of Papa's flock when he got sick, just to buy food. So he treated Javen like a man and offered him a business proposition. Javen agreed.

Later~The Story of Smashing Idols

When Abram left, my brother sat across from me at our little table and told me things so wondrous I don't want to forget them.

There was a gleam in Javen's eyes before he even began. "Rhoda," he said, "Abram is a follower of the one true God. Abram has even heard God's voice. God promised to make Abram into a great nation, and God promised to bless him. Someday Abram's name will be great, and he'll be known everywhere!"

I already knew that Papa would want us to be with Abram and Sarai. Not long before Papa died, he took me outside and we walked to our favorite olive tree. Papa never pruned that tree. He loved its wildness. So that ancient olive tree had grown to at least sixteen cubits tall. That's five Papas stacked on top of one another! I remember how the tree's oldest boughs were spread low and wide to allow for the younger branches and new shoots to sprout from the very center. I loved the fine shade beneath those branches and how already they were heavy with clusters of green, unripened olives. I told Javen about that day—how Papa bent down and brushed the fallen olives from the weedy grass below. How he patted the dirt and motioned for me to join him on the ground. Papa's normally brown and sun-weathered skin had lost some of its color. He was pale, and I knew he didn't feel well. His gentle, brown eyes lacked their usual luster.

So I sat beside him and waited in the silence while he tugged on his gray beard. I'd seen him do this whenever he was troubled or in deep thought.

"There's something I want you to remember," Papa said. He said my name slowly, then spoke calmly, but I sensed what he was going to tell me was important, something he felt he didn't have much time to say—something I should never forget. "I should've talked to you about this long ago," Papa said, "but I didn't because of your mother."

He pointed to the metal charm I wore around my neck—a metal square engraved with a crescent moon and hung on a leather string. The necklace had belonged to my mother when she was alive. She wore it to ward off evil spirits. I didn't know much about evil spirits, but the necklace reminded me of Mama, and I felt like I still had part of her with me by wearing it. When she died, I'd asked Papa if I could have the charm. The day Papa and I sat beneath the olive tree I wondered if he wanted it back. I reached up to finger it protectively.

"Your mother was raised to believe in the existence of many gods," Papa said. "We all were. As you know, people here worship gods called Nanna and Utu."

Papa no longer called Nanna and Utu "our gods." I noticed this right away. *But why?* I'd wondered then. Nana is the moon god, and Utu, her son, is the god of the sun and order and justice. Mama had taught me that. She used to pull me outside when the sky was black and the moon was full and bright. "Look close," she'd say and point to the heavens. "Sometimes Nanna will fly through the sky as a white bull."

Papa interrupted my memories then. "Rhoda," he said, more serious than I'd ever heard him before, "I don't believe there is a Nanna or an Utu. I don't believe in the existence of Iskur, the storm god, and all of the other ones."

I clutched the charm tighter in my hand.

"I know," I told him. "I heard you and Abram talk. You believe in the one God Abram tells of."

Javen smiled as I told this. I contined to recount the day . . .

"Yes," Papa agreed, "I do. There's something special about Abram that I can't explain to you. He seems to know things the rest of us don't. He asks questions that you and I wouldn't know to ask. I trust him. If he says there's one God, then I believe there's one God."

I told Javen how Papa and I sat beneath that olive tree for the next hour and Papa told me a story. Papa stretched out his legs in front of him and leaned against the wide, gnarled trunk of the great tree. His toes peeked out of his worn leather sandals, and I remember noticing how his feet were heavily calloused. He said:

"When Abram was just a boy, Terah, his father, owned an idol shop. The little shop was filled with wooden statues of the gods. One day, Terah needed to go somewhere and told Abram to mind the store.

"Abram went inside and studied the idols sitting on the dusty shelves. He decided to give an offering of grain to the largest one. He placed it in a small mound and left for a short while. When he returned, he saw that the wooden god had not touched the offering.

"'What kind of a god is this?' he asked aloud. 'I leave him an offering and he doesn't consume it in fire? Why, he hasn't even touched it. This is no god. It's a statue carved from wood by the hands of a man.'

"Abram took a hammer and smashed all of the idols except the largest one. He put the hammer near that one and waited. When his father returned, he told him that the large idol had smashed the others.

"Terah was very angry. 'That's nonsense,

Abram!' he shouted. 'Everyone knows that idols can't speak, let alone move about.'

"'Father,' Abram beseeched him, 'let your ears hear what your tongue speaks.'"

Javen smiled and nodded his head. "Papa was wise to tell you this," he said.

"That's what Papa said," I told Javen. I explained how Papa was silent after telling me the story, how the only sound was of the olive tree branches rattling softly in the wind and Papa's breath heaving in and out of his parted lips. Only then had he said, "Rhoda, Abram is right. Why do we worship idols that can't move, don't speak, and don't accept offerings?"

I had no answer, but Papa did.

"Abram has a wisdom that is not human," he said. "I believe in the existence of this one true, powerful God, and I believe he's chosen Abram to be his messenger on earth."

Papa reached over and opened my hand. He ran a rough finger over the charm. "Wear this if you want to remember your mother, as long as you know that it has no power. There's truth in the words Abram speaks, and there's power in the God he knows. I want you to know this God too."

Javen was quiet after I told him Papa's words. I was too. Yet it was as if we'd agreed: It was right for my brother to accept Abram's offer.

The more I think on this now, the more I wonder: Had Papa spoken to Abram before he died? It would be just like him to make sure we were cared for when he was gone.

We're Leaving Haran

Sarai said we can't take much with us when we leave—only two tunics each, a pair of sandals, and a few other personal items. She said not to worry about other things. She and Abram had plenty of bed mats and anything else we might need.

Sarai also instructed us that every item that could be rolled up should be—clothes, mats, tents, cloth to use for a variety of purposes. We were to stuff everything else into sacks that could be slung over the backs of the donkeys. Once I packed all of Dibri's and Javen's things, and my own, I went to help Sarai. Everyone was buzzing around her house. There were bags of grain, dried fruit, nuts, and little pouches of salt to secure to the donkeys. Dozens of fat water skins were filled and hung from each side of the animals. It's been a long day of work, and I'm so tired. Tomorrow we start for a new land. What waits for us there?

What a Strange Night!

I dreamt of Mama and Papa and woke feeling a little sad, but then not sad too. What is it? Maybe that one part of our lives is about to end, while another is just beginning. I'm afraid of the things ahead—the unknown—but excited at the same time about all the possibilities. Will we live by a city or in the wild? Will I find new friends? What will our new home be like?

Of course, I'm sad to leave the places that remind me of Mama, the places where we played together and sat gazing at the heavens together. I am terribly sad to leave behind my father's beautiful old olive tree, because it is a most special place to me.

I'm grateful, though, for Sarai and Abram. They're so good to us, and I feel safe with them. I believe there is something special about them. I'm not sure what it is, but they aren't like others I know. They seem always to think and talk of God. Somehow I believe what Papa told me, and what Javen agrees with: God will make Abram great. Maybe on this journey I'll get the chance to see some of this greatness.

Javen thinks so. I know he misses Papa, but Javen looks up to Abram in a way I've never seen him look up to anyone else.

I'll have to write about this more later. There's no time now. Abram and Sarai are calling all of us to get ready for our journey. The countryside is calling us too. A light dew has frosted the ground, and the sky is streaked with color.

Good-bye, little home. I love you. I will never forget all of the good times here with Mama and Papa. How I miss them. How I'll miss you!

The Land of Canaan ~ Shekhem

As we traveled today, our little home became just a silhouette in the sky. I kept wanting to look back, to memorize every bit of how our home looked. Even now, as we're taking a little rest to eat a bit of fruit and some olives, I wonder, *Will I ever return?*

But Abram has said all day, "Keep moving steadily." He led our procession, and his nephew Lot brought up the rear. I rode in between on a little donkey I shared with Dibri. Sarai rode a donkey too, as did two of her female maidservants who are always nearby. These maids are girls just a little older than me. I notice that Sarai likes to surround herself with us, with all the children. We like being around her too.

Javen doesn't want to be considered a child. Abram treats Javen like a man, which is fine with him. With the other boys in the household, my big brother rode behind the women and children and helped herd the goats, sheep, and a few oxen. I kept turning to look behind me as I bounced on my sweet donkey's back. Oh, for one last peek of the olive tree, of my little house, of my life as I have known it until now.

Sarai watched me do this a couple times. "Look ahead, Rhoda," she called finally. "Never look behind."

I smiled and nodded my head. Dibri was sleepy,

and the gentle motion of the ride made him close his eyes. He leaned against me, and after a while I could tell he'd fallen into a deep sleep. I knew he missed Papa and that he didn't understand where Papa had gone or why he wasn't coming back. But he's still little, and this adventure of getting to ride a donkey with all the adults is exciting to him, if a little tiring too.

After a while, we came to the ford of the Jabbok and crossed it with ease. The ford is a shallow stream at this point and could be crossed even on foot with no problem.

Then we moved south toward the Jordan River. I'd heard this was a strange and dangerous area, but I'd never been here. What I saw was swamp land, and I heard rumors of how it was filled with wild animals.

I didn't know about the animals, but there wasn't a sign of human life anywhere near. Sarai must have sensed how troubling this was, for she rode close to Dibri and me. She said it's very unusual to find a water source as large as the Jordan River that doesn't have camps and villages clustered on its banks.

We continued on in silence for a bit. Abram didn't stop to talk with Sarai as he moved to the back of our group. I turned to watch him move toward Javen and Lot. I could see him talking low, so I let my donkey lag back a bit so I could over-hear.

Abram urged Javen and Lot, "Stay close to the flocks. The tall grass and brush on the banks hide the lions' dens.

Earlier today I heard Abram's warnings: "There will be plenty of wild animals—lions, wolves—near the Jordan. We must find a path across between the rapids and then be out of the area as soon as possible."

Sarai missed me and let her camel lag back too. "Let's keep up," she encouraged. "Don't worry. We're in good hands."

I felt better riding near Sarai because she kept reminding me that Abram, Lot, and Javen each car-ried a sharp dagger. I looked back and saw the han-dles peeking out from the leather girdles they wore around their waists. Each girdle was supported by a strap of leather around one shoulder. Sarai was right. We were in good hands. She had told me that God was with us, that he had called Abram and all his household on this journey. That brought me comfort, but it looks like we're going to be on our way again. I don't think I can finish writing about how we crossed the Jordan.

Later

How tired I am! My bottom still hurts. As a matter of fact, my whole body is sore from the uncomfortable position I've ridden in all day because of Dibri. Never before have I so badly wanted my feet to touch the ground. I almost cried with relief when we stopped. I'm not used to riding a donkey for so long.

Dibri did cry when I lifted him down. He was tired and hungry and didn't know where he was. I think this will be the hardest part of our new life for him. Every day we will be in a new place. I don't think he or Javen or I realized how difficult this can be. Anyway, we're all full now, and Dibri has run off to find Javen.

Our dinner of dates, almonds, and bread was very good. The fruit and nuts are all around us. We roasted some of the nuts to take with us for later and have been collecting as many dates as possible.

We didn't reach this place, this oasis, until late in the day. Sarai said it's called Shekhem. I call it Paradise! It's a wonderful place to camp. The branches of these trees are so fat. They spread out far and wide and provide perfect shade. Clusters of almond trees surround the natural spring, and the date palms bulge with fruit. There's also a grove of enormous terebinth trees.

We can only spend one night here, Abram said, so there isn't time to set up the tents. But that's okay. It means less work as far as I'm concerned. I know I'll be able to sleep with or without a tent after all of the riding today!

Javen immediately led the flocks first to the spring to drink and then to an open area to graze. I gathered wood for the fire so we could have bread. I was deep in the grove picking up sticks when I saw Abram walk by. He knelt on the ground and pushed together a mound of dirt and large rocks. Then he walked away toward the flocks.

I wanted to follow him, but first I must tell you, little diary, about how we crossed the Jordan today. There is so much happening, after all, that if I don't write it down now, I will surely not have time to do so later!

We followed the course of the river for a good while. I saw the angry, swirling rapids and was glad Abram was our guide. It was hard to believe Dibri was still asleep, but his head had sunk into the crook of my arm, and he was snoring. I was thankful. I didn't want him to wake up right then and cry.

Finally, Abram decided it was safe to cross. We moved down the bank, and I could feel my little donkey's feet sink into the swampy murk. Then we crossed. All of the donkeys were hesitant, but at Abram's urging the animals stepped into the river and moved across quickly. The water was cool, and it swirled around my calves. I gripped my donkey's reins, afraid she'd sink into the river mud and take me down with her.

She didn't. She's very sure of her steps and never once hesitates or slows down unless I ask her. She climbed up the bank steadily to the other side.

Getting the other animals across was a different story. It took more time to cross the flocks. The sheep would follow Abram over a cliff, but the goats are more difficult. Javen, Lot, and a few boys had to walk on either side of the herds and stay back, bringing up the rear the whole way. When we all finally made it to the other side, there was a great clomping of hooves, then only the sound of the rushing rapids and an eerie quiet. I was glad to leave the Jordan, and even more glad when we came to a wadi that took us north again. Abram decided to follow the wadi, which is like a little stream. This time of year the wadis can be quite full from the winter rains or the springs that bubble up from underground. It's better to stay close to the water source, even if it means we must travel north again before we can go south, Sarai explained to me. During the hot months, even the wadis can dry up and turn to dusty little valleys that cut through the land.

Oh, there's Abram again. What's he doing out there in the flocks? It's so strange how he pushed that dirt and those rocks into a mound, and how he's still out there looking over all the animals. I'm going to pretend to pick up more sticks for our fires and see what he's up to . . . maybe Javen, out there with the sheep, will know.

Much, Much Later

I'm writing this in the moonlight. I'm so tired, but I must put down what happened. As I moved closer to Abram, I saw him pick up a beautiful lamb, one of the best in the flock, and carry it in his arms to the mound of dirt and rocks he'd made.

Then Abram reached for the knife at his side. My heart beat so fast I thought it would jump out of my throat. I inhaled sharply and dropped the sticks I'd been collecting. I bent down and pressed my hands over my ears until all I could hear was the rush of my own blood.

Moments later I inched my hands away from my head and listened. It was quiet. Only then did I gather up the dropped twigs and walk back to the camp. My heart was still beating fast as I searched quickly for Sarai.

I thought, *Where is she? What was Abram doing?*

But I couldn't find Sarai. Our camp is large, with all the servants and Lot's family. It seemed like a long time as I searched and searched for Sarai.

Then I saw Abram return. It was apparent to everyone that he was changed. His face shone, and his eyes were moist. People grew quiet.

I finally spotted Sarai coming back from playing with some of Lot's children. I ran to her, but she was walking to Abram. They sat down far from all of us and talked softly. They looked intent and serious, so I stayed back.

For a long time they were quiet. Finally, Sarai looked up and saw me watching them. She stood and smiled. She walked toward me but seemed far away in her thoughts.

"What is it?" I asked. "What has Abram been doing?"

Sarai smiled gently. "God appeared to him," she murmured. She looked across the horizon at all the country we'd crossed. "God told Abram that he would give this land to our offspring," she said.

"Abram made a mound of dirt and rocks," I told her. "I saw him as I gathered the sticks. Then he fetched a lamb and killed it. Why did he do that, Sarai? Why?"

Sarai reached over and stroked my hand. "Don't be afraid, child. That dirt and those rocks were an altar. Abram built an altar to God and gave him an offering. It was done to honor God and to remind him of the blessings he promised to Abram."

Sarai stared away again. She was lost in her thoughts.

I followed her eyes across the horizon, hoping it would help me understand.

She must've sensed my bewilderment.

"We can't begin to understand the mind of God," she said with a sudden smile. "Let's try to get some rest. We have to rise and travel again at day-break."

I'm now beside some of the maidservants. We've rolled out our mats and covered ourselves with cloaks, and the others have fallen asleep under the broad branches of the trees. Dibri has gone to sleep close to his brother. That's good, I think. Maybe Javen is taking the place of Papa for Dibri.

Though I'm tired, I can't sleep yet. It's not because I've set down my bed mat on a cluster of hard, raw dates. It's because so much has happened today to make me think. I'm wondering about what God told Abram. If God is going to give all this land to Abram and Sarai's offspring, won't they need children first? How can that be possible? Sarai is sixty-five years old already, and Abram is seventy-five. Perhaps Sarai was thinking about this too—about her age. I know how much she wants a child. She's spoken of it many times. She looks after us like we're her children. She even came to me tonight just before bed to make sure I was settled for the night.

Oh, how all this wondering makes me even more tired. I'm afraid it's enough for today.

It's Morning at the Oasis

I was awakened by a small hand rubbing my face. When I opened my eyes, Dibri's two black orbs peered back at me.

"I'm hungry," he announced. He may be looking up to Javen like he looked up to Papa, but he still comes to me for things like breakfast.

But that's okay. I was hungry too. I hugged him and rubbed my back before rolling up my sleeping mat.

Surprise—little dates! I forgot I'd slept on what turned out to be our breakfast. The good thing is my tossing and turning in the night had softened them a little. Dibri grabbed a handful with delight. I couldn't blame him. The sweet dates were too tempting to be left alone.

Dibri and I ate in the darkness, but all around us were the silhouettes of other people waking up and moving about the camp. A fire burned in the pit, and a smoky plume rose into the morning air.

It's cooler in the mornings, and a fire is always welcome. Within a short time, the air heats up and the dew burns off. Since we'd be traveling south now, I knew we were bound to run into soaring temperatures. I didn't look forward to that.

In all the morning hubbub, I spotted Sarai and watched her move toward the donkeys. She had a long shawl wrapped around her head and shoulders, and she moved with deliberation and grace. I got up and walked over to her.

"Rhoda!" Sarai greeted me with a smile. "How did you sleep on your first night away from your home?"

"I don't remember," I answered.

Sarai laughed. "Then you slept quite well," she said, laughing some more.

Her laugh always startles me. It's a rich, deep laugh that rolls out of her mouth with a sweetness to the ear, like honey is to the taste. It's a laugh that warms everyone who hears it. Though I'd recognize her laugh anywhere now, it always seems an unexpected surprise. Maybe it's because of the sadness that surrounds Sarai. Maybe that sadness grips her because of the offspring God has promised her but that she doesn't have . . . these are things I still wonder about.

"Come," Sarai said, interrupting my thoughts. "We'll prepare the food together. Gamilat and Pigat are stoking the fire for the bread."

Gamilat and Pigat are two of Sarai's maidservants whom I've ridden alongside and whom I slept near last night. Pigat is a small girl and very quiet. She moves about the camp with the agility of a leopard. She rises before anyone else and goes to sleep after everyone else. Did I mention that she's very efficient at everything she does? I admit I'm a bit jealous of her. If only I could be such a good helper!

Gamilat, on the other hand, is friendly and talkative and would rather stop and chat than do chores. I think that after we've been together for a while, we'll be good friends.

We work very well together, Gamilat, Pigat, and I. Sarai noticed this a few days ago, and now she comments on it every day.

Last night, we had fun as we did our work. I helped Gamilat make goat butter. We filled a skin with goats' milk and hung it between three sticks. We shook the bag, then squeezed it, shook the bag, then squeezed it, until the milk turned thick and a lumpy butter formed.

"When you have fun at your work it doesn't seem so much like work," Gamilat told me, laughing as we shook the bag and squeezed.

I thought about that today as I took a bag of barley flour from a pouch on one of the donkeys and Gamilat grabbed the bag of salt. I dumped flour into a bowl, and some of it poofed onto my nose and at Gamilat. We laughed at the sight of each other covered in the white powder! Then I added the water, and Gamilat the salt, into the bowl. She threw in a bit of fermented dough from yesterday, and I mixed it all with my hands.

As the fire died down, Pigat scraped the area clean with a wide, flat stick. I dropped a mound of the sticky dough onto the hot ground, and she covered it with burning embers. A short while later, she scraped away the embers and moved the browned bread cakes to a flat stone to cool.

When Sarai saw how efficiently we'd prepared the meal, she called the men together. They sat on several long, leather cloths spread out on the dirt. We laid out the food as Sarai smiled at us. Then we all fell silent, and Abram offered a blessing.

He said, "Blessed are you, Adonai our God, ruler of the universe, who brings forth bread from the earth."

Then there was a moment of silence before we all began to eat. All the women and children ate on another cloth spread out nearby the men. We smeared our bread with goat butter and ate cheese curds, dates, olives, and walnuts. I was so hungry. Food had never tasted so good. We washed it all down with goats' milk.

Most everyone has finished eating now, so I must help clean and get ready. Sarai says whatever we unpacked last night must be packed up again. Then we'll set off once more on our journey.

Lunch

We've stopped for a little rest, and so that the men can eat a little. They're working so hard to keep all the flocks and oxen together.

Our donkeys need watering too. I have a few minutes to write while Naamah drinks.

Did I record earlier, little diary, that I've decided to call my donkey Naamah? The name means "sweetness" in Hebrew, and she really is very sweet. After how she carried us through the Jordan, I've come to trust her to deliver Dibri and me across whatever is ahead.

Oh, and about names, today I learned what mine means today— "rose" in Hebrew! Sarai told me. She said children are always given names that suit their character or personality. I asked Javen about this, and he remembered Mama saying that I was red like a rose when I was born, and she said I was precious to her like a rose is precious.

I think she must have added that last part just to make me feel special!

I asked Javen what his name means. He said, "clay." He told me that Dibri's name means "promise of the Lord."

Mama didn't have a chance to give Dibri his name before she died, Javen told me, so Papa did. Papa told Javen that God had promised him one more child before he took Mama home. Papa wanted to remember that every time he called Dibri.

God sure makes a lot of promises.

I thought about that as I bounced along today with Dibri in front of me again. I thought about all of our names too. It helped pass the time and was an interesting distraction.

I still don't know for sure what *Abram* means. Javen thought "high father," but he didn't know for sure. He'll try to find out, he said.

We all know what Sarai's name means: "princess." Abram calls her this sometimes. She certainly looks like how a princess might. Sarai has long, chocolate brown hair and a clear, fair complexion. She's beautiful.

I wonder what I'll look like when I'm sixty-five years old. I'll be grateful if I look a fraction as beautiful.

Making Camp ~ Bethel

We followed the watershed south all day until we came to an area of brush-covered and forested hills. Abram thought it was a good place to water the animals again and let them feed. It was decided that we'd make camp for at least a few days.

I've wondered since we set out where we'll eventually settle. Sarai calls this land "Canaan," which is where I thought we were going. Of course, the land of Canaan is very large. Is it possible that Abram wants to explore all of it before he settles on a home? I hadn't thought about that before! Maybe he'll decide to move us from place to place. He's a shepherd, after all, and shepherds are nomads.

Oh, I'm tired, and this isn't a pleasant thought . . . but wait!

I just saw Abram walk off again. I think he'll make another altar to God.

Sarai told me Abram wants to make altars to the Lord wherever he goes. Abram believes that if he spends time with God, he will have God's protection, and his whole household will be protected too. Sarai said a home, even it's a camp, should be a place of love, beauty, comfort, and warmth. It can be none of those things without God's protection.

When I hear Sarai talk, I'm reminded of Papa. I know how pleased he would be to hear her teaching me like he tried to do. He wanted his children to know more about the one true God, and he wanted them to draw close to God. I remember his words under the olive tree: "There's power in the God whom Abram knows. I want you to know this God too."

I hope he knows somehow that his prayer has been answered. I see how Abram and Sarai follow God, and I realize something else. It isn't just that they follow, but that God is leading. He is leading all of us. He has brought us across the Jordan. He has provided the water for our animals, and even all those delicious dates and almonds. He is providing a way for us.

So it looks like we'll be here for a little while. We unfolded our tents, and the men pounded in the poles that supported each tent. Then pegs were driven into the ground to secure the ropes from each tent covering. Lot directed all of this activity and had the men set the tents in an inner circle first, surrounded by two larger ones. The larger tents belong to Abram and Sarai, and there are several tents for Lot and his household. The smaller tents are for the servants. And then there are more tents for the littlest children, like Dibri. Sarai loves to spend time in that tent with the children. She delights in them!

Each tent has a curtain that hangs down from the top of the entrance. And this brings me back to where I began writing today, sitting in the tent I share with Pigat and Gamilat.

Right now the door flap is rolled up to let in the nice breeze. The walls of our tent are lifted up as well. When we go to sleep, we'll pull them back down to discourage animals from sleeping with us—or worse, attacking us. I'm always a little bit afraid to keep my tent open at any time, but Sarai assures me that I'm fine.

Did I mention we had a special treat for our supper?

Javen noticed a flock of quail in the bushes nearby. He caught at least ten of them in a special snare he made. We roasted them on sticks over the fire. It's the first bit of meat we've eaten since we left Haran, and it was a welcome supper.

Abram sits in the entrance to his tent. He may

call Sarai his princess, but Sarai calls him the king of the camp because he sits at his tent door like a king sits on his throne! She laughs her musical laugh when she teases him about this. The truth is, from his vantage point Abram can watch over his household and keep an eye out for weary travelers.

I was told it's a rare traveler who isn't welcomed by Abram. Gamilat told me the tent curtains are pulled up most of the time to welcome travelers. They're often hungry and thirsty and in need of shade and rest. When travelers enter the camp, they're under the protection of the camp. This is part of an unspoken code practiced by nomads like us.

Since we're camped on a forested hill, the wind sings a little song as it moves through the branches of the trees. There's a tiny cricket that sits beside me now. He's brave to hop out of the bushes and into my tent. His brothers and sisters are afraid. They'll only sing from the shadows.

I hear the laughter of the children now. Sarai must be with them again, playing some game or helping settle them on their mats for sleep. I can always pick out Dibri's voice from the crowd of crying boys and girls. Tonight he's quiet, and I hope that means he's asleep!

I feel safe and protected here, but I also feel lonesome and sad. I've noticed that I don't feel this way during the day. There's so much activity, and the sun is a bright and cheerful friend. But the night is so quiet. It digs deep into my thoughts and exposes all of my fears.

From My Tent

When the dawn came this morning, I realized this was the first time I've awakened inside a tent. The morning rays slipped through the goat-hair walls and woke me up in a gentle, peaceful way.

I kept on my old tunic and went to find Sarai. I wanted to bathe myself, but I hadn't brought anything to use. I was sure she must have something. I passed Abram as he sat in the entrance of his tent.

"Boker tov," he greeted me, with a lopsided smile. His beard was long and gray, and it fell to his chest.

"Good morning," I greeted him back and smiled.

I stood outside Sarai's tent and called her name

softly. "Come in, Rhoda," she said. Her long hair was swept over her shoulder. She was finishing braiding it, one hand and then the other pulling the hair over and under.

"Sarai, I wondered if you had anything to wash with—I'd like to clean myself this morning," I told her.

She finished her hair, walked to the side of her tent, and reached into a pouch. A small cloth was tied up with string, and she opened it carefully. "Here are some plant ashes," she said. "I'm sure you know what to do. Mix them with a bit of the olive oil stored in the skin outside."

She smiled as I took the ashes from her. Back in Haran, we used to mix them with animal fat, but olive oil works well too.

Pigat and Gamilat joined me. We gathered the soiled clothes around the camp on our way toward a tiny stream. At the stream we each took an armful of tunics and submerged them in the cold, cold water. We rubbed the clothes together to work out any dirt and stains, then wrung out each garment again and again. We hung every piece of clothing on the branches of the trees to dry.

Then we each pinched some ashes into our hands, poured a few drops of oil over them, and mixed the ashes with our fingers. We rubbed the mixture over our faces and necks and on our arms and legs. We reached everywhere we could, and then we rinsed with the cool water.

We sat on the bank, and Gamilat laughed. "I think this is what it must be like to have sisters," she said.

Pigat was quiet and didn't say anything.

"I've never had sisters either," I said. "What happened to your family, Gamilat?"

She shrugged. "I was sold so my parents could offer a dowry for my older brother's bride." I was startled by her bluntness.

I must've appeared shocked, because Pigat spoke up. "It happens all the time. Girls who are young and healthy go for a fair price in the market. It happened to me too. My family sold me to pay off a debt. This is the third household I've been in since I turned eight."

I didn't know what to say. They already knew about Mama and Papa. I told them the story when I met them. Now, though still sad my parents were dead, I felt fortunate that they had never sold me. How sad that would have been. I felt bad for my friends who had been sold by their parents—just as bad as someone would feel if they came from a wealthy home and their friends didn't. I wasn't used to these feelings.

I think Gamilat sensed this, because she smiled and took my hand, and Pigat's too. "I suppose this is our home now," she said, swinging our arms into the air. "So maybe we really are like sisters."

Pigat looked at me and smiled too. "I'll be the big, bossy sister because I think I'm older than you. I'm eleven. How old are you, Rhoda?"

"Seven," I told them.

"Well, you can't be the big sister, Pigat, because you know I'm older than you," Gamilat said. "I'm twelve!" She sat down between Pigat and me and put her arms around us. There was something light and breezy about Gamilat, and that comforted me. Pigat may be a year younger than Gamilat, but she sure seems like the wise, older sister. I like that too.

I wonder what they think of me.

Later

We walked back together, and I went into my tent to change my tunic. It's tan color with stripes of green and blue looked brighter after being cleaned. I saw Dibri's head pop through the curtain. It popped back out when he saw me.

"Shoo!" I said. "I'm still dressing."

I heard a sniffle then, and I felt bad. *I could've been kinder to him,* I chided myself. When I went outside, Dibri was crouched in the dirt. Tears streamed down his dirty face. "What is it?" I asked and bent down beside him.

"I want to go home. I miss Papa, and I miss our home," he sobbed.

I put my arms around his little body and squeezed him close to me. "I miss him too," I told him. That was all I could say. The only thing that would make him feel better would be for Papa to come home. I knew that wasn't going to happen.

"Come on," I said, "let's get something to eat. Then you can go and see about the flocks with Javen."

"I don't want to see about the flocks," he said. "Those goats always eat my tunic."

I laughed and mussed up his mop of thick, black hair. "Then see about the sheep," I told him. "Anyway, how will you ever become a fine shepherd if you don't show those goats who's boss. Did Javen make you a staff yet?"

"No," Dibri complained.

I knew Javen's typical response by now: "I'm working on it." Poor Dibri! Javen might be working on it for fifty years!

"Well," I said. "Maybe he'll have it finished today. Let's go see."

Dibri and I walked away from the tents and beneath some bushy trees. We picked up as much kindling as we could carry and stacked it beside the woodpile on the outside of camp. We saw Pigat and Gamilat as they hauled bags of water from the spring.

Sarai spread out several pieces of cloth and put pieces of hot bread in all of them. She added small chunks of goats' cheese and several dried dates. Then she tied up each one with a string.

"Here, Dibri," she called. "Abram has gone into the field. Lot is there, and so are Javen and the boys. Bring them something to eat, and I'll have a special treat for you when you return."

Dibri ran off with a big smile on his face. Sarai always gives him special little treats. Walnuts soaked in honey are his favorite.

There's Drought in Canaan

It's so hot! I can't sit and write in the tent anymore tonight, so I've moved outside. Though it's evening, the heat is still with us. Even the sky is lit with hot colors. A deep reddish glow lights the horizon.

The heat grows more intense with each day that passes. Every morning Abram stands in the middle of camp and looks upward for a sign of rain, but there is none. In the day, the sky is vast and blue. There isn't even a wisp of cloud. The springs are drying up, and the grass is turning brown.

After supper, Lot came into camp and talked to Abram at the entrance to his tent. They talked for quite a while, and when Lot left, Abram went into Sarai's tent.

Pigat and I were cleaning up in the camp when Gamilat found us. "I think we'll have to move on," she told us. "Lot talked to Abram. He said the grasses are withering, and soon the flocks won't have anything to eat. Abram calls it a famine."

I had heard Papa talk about how a famine meant all the water would dry up, and all the people, plants, and animals with it. "Oh no," I cried. "What do you think will happen? Is there somewhere we can go?"

"We can go back north," Pigat suggested. "Or I suppose we can go south."

"South?" I asked. "What's south? I thought the Negev was south."

The Negev is a huge desert, and everyone knows about the desert! During the summer months, the desert heat can be unbearable, and there's very little water. How would going south, into the desert, help? I was confused. Heading south didn't make any sense unless we were going to Egypt.

At that moment Sarai walked out of her tent and headed toward us. "Abram thinks it's wise for us to move on," she said. "He's heard from some travelers that there's plenty of food in Egypt. We must get packed up again. He wants to leave at daybreak."

Gamilat, Pigat, and I were stunned! Then we were busy like ants packing up camp for another journey.

So tomorrow we are to travel through the Negev. There's no other way to Egypt.

In the Negev

I haven't had a chance to write again until now, my little diary. We left seven days ago at daybreak, and each day we don't stop until late in the afternoon. Abram said the journey to Egypt should take about fourteen days. If he's right, then we're halfway there.

The Negev is hotter and drier than I ever imagined a place could be. The rolling hills just north abruptly give way to endless stretches of dirt and rock and parched white limestone. It's a shocking, formidable sight.

We travel along what Javen tells me is the Way to Shur. It's a direct route through the Negev, and nomads like us often use it. We've already passed several Bedouin camps. They're the true desert dwellers. From far away their black goat-hair tents look like little ants dotting the dirt.

Trade caravans also use this land route to bring goods north or south. I get more of my information from snatches of conversation I overhear between

Abram and Lot than from Javen. My brother can be very silent, and he keeps things Abram tells him to himself. But that's okay. I've learned to stay quiet and keep my ears open. It's the best way to learn things.

We stop at every oasis we come to along the way, but there aren't many of them. The ones that do exist aren't at all like the ones in the north. The springs here at an oasis in the Negev are scanty, but at least there's been enough water to refill our skins and allow the animals to drink. I don't always understand it, but I believe Sarai is right: God does provide.

There are acacia trees here and there that provide a bit of shade. Sometimes I see cloth or rugs hanging from the branches of these trees. There's no other visible sign of human habitation near them. No tents, no donkeys, no people anywhere.

The first time I saw the rugs hanging in the trees, I stared at the curious sight until my head was almost swiveled in its socket. Sarai saw me, and she laughed. She does that a lot. She finds joy at the most unusual times and laughter in the most unusual places. This joy seems to bring her so much pleasure, and it cheers the rest of us too.

"You have a marvelous curiosity," Sarai said amid laughter at my bewildered expression. "That acacia you observe is very holy to the Bedouins," she explained. "A vow taken beneath the arms of the tree can't be broken. When the Bedouins move to other grazing grounds, they hang their extra belongings from the branches of the acacia for storage. They believe that no one would steal anything from the boughs of the sacred tree."

We haven't set up our tents since we entered the Negev. We stop so late in the day and leave so early that Abram says there's no point. We eat one big meal just after we stop and build a fire. Usually it consists of bread, figs, dates, nuts, and olives. Locusts are plentiful, and sometimes Sarai roasts them. Abram seems to enjoy them, but they're not my favorite.

In any case, it's been interesting moving through the desert. Today several trade caravans passed us. There were twenty-five camels carrying goods north from Egypt. Another fifteen camels carried perfumes and spices from Somalia and Arabia. They slowed down to take a look at us, and Abram stopped to talk with the men leading the caravan. When the camel drivers began to gawk at Sarai, we left, and Abram quickened our pace.

I never forget how beautiful Sarai is, but the way newcomers react to her is a good reminder for anyone else who might take her beauty for granted!

For the most part, Dibri has been very good. He seems to be both fascinated by the Negev and startled by its bareness. We've already learned an important lesson: The desert reveals unexpected surprises and hidden pleasures to those who are patient.

We were startled to see a group of wild goats walking single file along a steep, sandstone cliff. Another day two gazelles eyed us with genuine curiosity as they munched on the boughs of an acacia tree. Lizards often scurry past us on the desert road, and it's not uncommon to see herds of wild donkeys.

Once Dibri spotted a lone camel. Abram told us it had probably belonged to the Bedouins at one time. They let their sick or old camels loose to fend for themselves.

I've decided that while the Negev is a most unusual place, it's not without its allure.

Our First Dust Storm

It was the middle of the afternoon yesterday when Abram stopped without warning and stared toward the west. Dibri saw something too. He pointed at the sky.

"Look at how dirty it is," he said.

The sky is dirty? I thought. But Dibri was right. The sky just above the horizon was brown, and I'd smelled dust in the air for the last hour or so. I looked at Sarai and could see she was concerned and tense. Her normally smooth face was wrinkled with concern, her mouth pursed, and her jaw tight. She kept scanning the sky around us.

Pigat and Gamilat were concerned and nervous too.

"What is it?" I whispered.

"A dust storm," Sarai answered for them. "We won't have time to put up our tents. Quickly! Wrap your scarf around your nose and mouth."

She pulled her own scarf from her head and gave it to me. "Wrap this around Dibri. You must move fast. He won't be able to breathe soon if you don't."

She swung her donkey around and scanned the

horizon. We spotted a group of black tents southeast of us, and Sarai rode over to Abram and pointed them out.

He nodded and called to Javen and Lot. "Gather the donkeys and stay in the rear."

Then he walked ahead of us. We quickened our pace and followed him. The wind was picking up, and I couldn't understand why the donkeys had to stay in the back; surely we could get there much faster by donkey than on foot. I asked Sarai about it.

She said, "The Bedouins believe that God created donkeys out of the earth," she shouted above the din of the wind. "They're considered a lower form of life. You should never approach a Bedouin camp on a donkey."

Several men rushed toward us as we neared the tents. They wore loose robes and white head cloths held in place by double black cords. With a flick of the hand, they summoned others in their camp to help with our flocks.

I heard one of the men exchange words with Abram. I knew they were speaking Aramaic. I used to hear it spoken in the marketplace in Haran. The men speaking Aramaic helped Lot and Javen lead the flocks to a sheltered pen between two sandstone bluffs.

Sarai was right. The wind whipped the blowing dust against my skin. I couldn't even see the horizon anymore, and the air suddenly was clouded with flying dirt, dust, and sand. My eyes burned, and even with the scarf wrapped around my mouth and nose, it was hard for me to breathe.

I felt someone grab my hands, but I couldn't see anything. When I tried to open my eyes wide, they were stung with sand and I squeezed them shut. I was helped through a wall of blowing sand, as was Dibri, and we were pulled along. I heard the familiar rustle of a tent flap and felt the quiet protection of it. I rubbed my eyes and slowly opened them.

Two Bedouin women stared back at me. Their long-sleeved dresses fell to their ankles, and their hems and sleeves were embroidered with colorful thread. Their hair was covered with black head cloths, and their long veils hid their faces. The veils were also embroidered and decorated with gold and silver coins.

The tent was divided by curtains into sections, and colorful rugs were spread on the ground. I couldn't see what was beyond one curtain, but I heard the voices of women and children who spoke Aramic too. None of us could understand the Bedouins' words, so they used their hands to tell us to sit down.

The walls of the tent billowed, and I began to feel nervous. Pigat was seated beside me. "Do you think we'll be all right here?" I whispered to her. "I mean, in the tent? Is it strong enough?"

She nodded and leaned close to my ear. "Look," She pointed to the poles above us. "They place the tent over the poles so the wind moves over its A-frame, instead of going through it. We're very safe here."

Dibri began to whimper, and one of the women smiled at him and disappeared behind the curtain. She appeared a moment later with a child who looked to be the same age. The child offered Dibri a piece of bread, and a moment later Dibri ran behind the curtain with him. I thought this must be the area where the children ate and played.

The men sat with us, and before long the women served supper. There were bowls of rice topped with a type of butter called *ghee*. There was also mutton, yogurt, and round loaves of unleavened bread. I noticed they didn't touch the food until they had served us first.

It was a delicious meal! I hadn't realized how hungry I was until those first bites. We drank camels' milk and ate sweet figs for dessert.

Sarai told me later that Bedouins would offer their guests a rich, delicious meal even it meant they had to kill their last sheep to do it. They're a very generous people.

The Bedouin women built a fire in a sand pit and made coffee. Each woman wore silver bracelets that reflected the firelight. The bracelets were inlaid with different colored stones, and I found myself staring at them.

One of the women came over to me and held up her wrist. She took my hand and ran it over the polished stones. Then she pointed to a red stone and turned to speak with Abram. I didn't understand, but he nodded his head.

"She wants me to explain the meaning of the stones," he said to me. "She sees that you are an admirer of beauty. The red stone she points to is coral. It imparts wisdom to the wearer."

She pointed to another stone, a beautiful blue one like the oasis water. "This one is turquoise," he explained. "It glows when the wearer is happy, but it becomes dull if the wearer is sad. The green one is worn to prevent disease." She pointed to the other stones, and each time Abram patiently translated.

It was cozy and comfortable in this shadowy Bedouin tent even though I could hear the wind raging outside. The tent walls shake with the sand that must be beating against them.

After a while, one of the men stood up; he was silhouetted on the wall of the tent. His shadow crept onto the ceiling. He spoke in Aramaic, but his voice was light and lyrical. I found out later that he'd recited a poem. The Bedouins often tell legends, sing songs, or recite poems while they drink their coffee. These stories, songs, and poems have been passed down through generations of Bedouin families.

I am to sleep on a rug this evening, wedged between Dibri on one side and Sarai, Gamilat, and Pigat on the other. I wanted to write all of this down before I forget it. I'm so tired, I know I'll never remember everything tomorrow. But Sarai is whispering that it's time to put down my pen. We're in the room behind the curtain, separated from the men. I can hear the quiet breathing of those around me. Once or twice the lonely howl of a wolf pierces the night, but no one is stirring. Sarai is right. It's time for me to sleep too. Good night, little diary.

A Bedouin Gift

I've learned that the Bedouins arrange their tents north to south. They believe that if they see the sunrise when they awaken, they'll have good luck. If I believed in the sun like they do, I might be the luckiest girl in the world! But then maybe not. I keep remembering what Papa said: The God of Abram—of Papa and Javen and now of me—is the most powerful.

In any case, this morning the sun peeked through the tent and nudged me with its pink rays until I opened my eyes. It took a moment for me to realize where I was. This has happened almost every morning since I left Haran.

The Bedouin men gathered our animals and brought them to us. The women gave us bundles of bread and figs for the remainder of our journey. As we climbed on the backs of our donkeys and prepared to leave, one of the women ran out of the tent. It was the same one who showed me her bracelet last night. Her robe billowed around her as she ran, and she put her hand on top of her head to keep her veil from flying away. She held up a silver bracelet with coral stones and smiled.

Pigat and Gamilat were next to me.

"It's a gift," Pigat said. "You should take it or you may insult her."

I took it from her fingers and intended to smile my appreciation, but as soon as the bracelet left her hand, she was gone.

Abram thanked the men, and we left. As we moved south, I continued my habit of looking behind me. Before long the Bedouin tent that had appeared in our moment of dire need faded behind us. It became another black dot in the endless stretch of desert.

I felt a pang of sadness until Sarai rode beside me. "Look ahead, Rhoda," she encouraged.

She's right. The view ahead is always better.

Desert Mirage

It's several days since we left the good company of our Bedouin friends. We've found another oasis and have stopped for the evening. There's enough water to refill our skins for the day ahead, but only if we continue to ration. Abram said we should reach Egypt by tomorrow afternoon.

Since I heard the good news, I haven't stopped thanking God. Like Abram and Sarai, I believe it's God who provides these things.

We're all so tired and hungry. If it weren't for the bread and figs given to us by the Bedouins, there would be even less in our stomachs right now. Our food supply is scant, and our water has been worse than that for the last two days. Dibri has drunk more than usual because of the soaring temperatures. He's gone through his own skin of water and most of mine. As a result, I'm not feeling well. My head hurts, and sometimes I'm dizzy.

Several times I thought I'd spotted a lake just ahead of us. "Look, Gamilat!" I'd cry and point in excitement.

She'd strain her neck and squint her eyes.

"What?" Gamilat would ask, peering round.

"What do you see, Rhoda?"

"It's a lake of some sort," I'd say and point to it again. "Right there! Can't you see it?"

She'd shake her head and look at me with a furrowed brow. "All I see is more dirt and rock. I don't think you're well."

"I don't think so either," Pigat would agree. "I've never heard of a lake in the middle of the Negev. It's just a mirage."

But I'd shake my head. *It's right there*, I'd think, *in plain sight*. How could they not see it? I'd look around me, but no one else seemed very excited by the prospect of a huge supply of fresh drinking water. What was wrong with everyone? When we'd pass the spot where I thought I'd seen the lake, I'd think, *What's wrong with me?*

All day long we pushed forward, and all day long the water was just out of reach. I couldn't understand it. If we covered an acre, the lake nudged ahead an acre. I had to agree finally: Pigat and Gamilat were right. I was seeing nothing more than a mirage.

The Negev is a cruel and merciless place.

How do the Bedouins do it, surviving out here

in the desert lands? I thought about this as Namaah bounced us along. I had renewed admiration for the Bedouins.

By the time we set up camp, my water skin container was dry as a bone. We ate a little, and everyone set up their mats and rested. Sarai says I must stop writing now and rest too. It's important to conserve our strength.

Today We're Near Egypt

I thought Egypt would promise good things. However, a pall has been cast upon our journey. I feel tired and dizzy because of the lack of water, food, and rest, but because of other things too . . .

We traveled along a narrow stretch of land today. A long arm of the Red Sea was south of us, and the Great Sea was to our north. If we continued west, we would enter directly into Egypt, Abram said. I was anxious to leave the Negev, and though both seas were a distance away, I was sure I smelled the salt in the breeze.

My throat was parched from the dry, dusty air. Abram would lead us to water, I was sure, but I wished it would be sooner rather than later.

We did pass a small lake to our right—a real one! Sarai said it was most likely part of the Red Sea before the waters receded south. Now this lake marks the border between the Negev and Egypt. I wanted to run and splash in it and drink from it. But just as I was about to knee Namaah to take off for the waters, I heard movement on my right.

I turned to see Abram. He rode past me on a donkey and joined Sarai just ahead. They rode side by side in silence for a long moment. Abram's serious face made me stay near and listen close.

"What is it?" Sarai finally asked her husband. "Tell me what troubles you."

Abram's sigh was heavy. "Sarai, my princess," he said, "you're a beautiful woman. Your eyes are like jewels, your skin like a creamy sea pearl."

She looked at him quizzically and laughed her musical laugh. "You needn't have come to tell me this, Abram," she said. "You've been my most ardent admirer for many years. There must be more. Tell me. What is it?"

I fear for my life," Abram said finally. "The Egyptians are not accustomed to beauty such as yours. When they see you, they'll want you. When they discover that I'm your husband, they'll surely kill me but let you live. I've come to make a request of you, dear wife."

They rode in silence again for what seemed a long time. The landscape evolved as we traveled west. Little bushes popped up here and there. Clumps of green grass and plants replaced the dead rock and dry sand.

Sarai spoke with a sudden intensity. "Abram, you've been my faithful husband for many years. You've stayed by my side even though I fail to conceive a child for you. There isn't a request you could make that I could refuse. Tell me now. What would you have me do?"

Abram looked at her with tenderness. "Tell them, Sarai, that you're my sister. If you tell them this, they'll let me live. They'll treat me well for your sake."

I saw Sarai turn her head. She stared away for a long time, and then I heard her quiet reply: "Very well."

The sadness in her voice made me start up on little Namaah.

Abram too was struck by it. He pulled back, and Sarai and all of us girls rode on in silence. Eventually, some of the girls started chatting again, but Sarai didn't say another word. I was troubled. Why would Abram tell her to lie?

Gamilat and Pigat had heard Abram's request too.

"Don't you know what this means?" Pigat whispered to me.

I shook my head.

"It means Abram thinks Pharaoh will want her when he sees her," she explained.

"Well, he can't just take her, can he?" I asked.

"It's not like that," Pigat said. "The king doesn't have to take anyone. Don't you see. No one refuses him. It's just not done. Not unless you want to anger the gods."

"Their gods?"

"You're in Egypt now," Pigat said, though not meanly. "Get used to it."

I must've looked shocked, but I knew Pigat had lived with an Egyptian family for a time. She had to know what she was talking about.

Pigat explained, "The Egyptians have many

gods, and they believe Pharaoh is the mediator between them and the gods. If you want to please the gods, and want to keep your life, you'd better please Pharaoh."

Suddenly Papa's words rang in my ears: "The one true God is the all powerful God." I felt new resolve. I had no intention of pleasing any gods except the one true God.

What troubles me, as I reflect on our day, is why Abram doesn't feel the same way. Isn't he the one who'd smashed idols—untrue gods—in his father's shop when he was just a boy? Why was he afraid of Egypt's untrue gods? Why would he allow Sarai to pose as his sister and not his wife?

Yesterday Egypt held so much promise. I daydreamed of water and food, mystery, and adventure. I carried in my memory the tales of Egypt that were told in the marketplace of Haran . . .

Every few months, the caravans of towering camels sauntered into town. They carried snowy-white linen cloth, sheets of papyrus, bulging sacks of barley and wheat. Dark-skinned merchants with missing teeth told about enormous pyramids that stab the azure sky and a river with no beginning that flows backwards.

Now I'm sorry we've come here. Mostly, I'm disappointed by Abram's words.

Water! At Last!

We're stopped for a little while to allow the animals to drink. First I had my share of the cool, cool water. Oh, how refreshing it is.

The sun has tilted west as the Nile Delta spreads before us like a lush, green fan. Abram signaled us to move forward to this branch of the Nile, but not before I'd spotted the pyramids and the great sphinx. The sphinx reared out of the desert dust like hooded cobras; they looked terrifying to me, even at a distance.

But I cannot think of them now. I want to enjoy this respite and the breeze from across the waters. By the way, the stories I heard in the marketplace in Haran were right! The water flows north instead of south. I couldn't believe it. Javen was with the flocks, and I ran to him.

"Look!" I said. "It's true. Look at the how the water flows!"

"I know," he said. "It's very strange. It flows north into the Great Sea. No one knows where the headwaters are." He pointed downstream. "Rhoda, we could follow this river forever and probably never find the source. I've heard it said that the river is wrapped around the whole earth."

Dibri ran through the clumps of blue-green reeds that sprouted on the banks. They towered over him like giants and flapped against one another in the light breeze. "There's a frog!" he shouted and dashed away. I ran to reach for him, and my sandals sank into the soppy, black soil.

"Rhoda," Sarai called to me, "don't let him run loose. There are crocodiles in the river."

I gulped and ran between the thick stalks, both of my feet sinking into the cool mud. Twice I stumbled and almost fell into the Nile. I just didn't have my strength back. I heard Dibri's laugh, and he unwittingly ran into me, squeezing a little frog in one hand.

I grabbed his arm and dragged him back.

Sarai laughed at our antics. It was the first time I'd seen her smile and heard her laugh since Abram whispered to her yesterday.

Of course, anyone would have to laugh seeing us. Dibri and I were splattered with black mud, and our feet and ankles were filthy.

"We must wash again soon," Sarai said. She turned serious and sad again. "Come. Abram is anxious to move on." So we bathed, and I have just enough time to scribble these notes before we move on.

Who knows what lies ahead. It looks promising. The river is to our right. To our left, there are fields of blue-flowering flax, maize, rice, and cotton. In the distance I can see inky canals that snake through the fields and water them. Pigat told me to look for the little girls who walk to the river. She remembered them most.

I see them now! The girls wrap their shawls around the crowns of their heads to balance clay pots on top. Who would imagine you could carry a heavy pot on your head? In any case, these girls are very graceful. It's so beautiful how they walk with the pots balanced on their heads to and from the river, disappearing through the tall stalks of maize.

"But beware, Pigat said. "The Egyptians believe creatures live in the river. The people call the creatures the 'owners of the Nile.'"

"Creatures?" I asked, a little scared.

"They're said to be half-human and half-fish, and they have long, slanted eyes." Pigat pulled her eyes back to show me the scary creature face. "Sometimes they fall in love with the humans who gather their water," she said, trying hard now to spook us. "Sometimes they even marry them."

Gamilat's eyes were wide.

"If you were to go with these girls down to the river," Pigat said, "you'd hear them address the creatures, 'With your permission, oh old and young.' Only then do the girls dare dip their pots into the Nile. They believe this gives the creatures a chance to scatter before they gather their water."

I pretended to not be scared by Pigat's accounts of Egypt, but I've decided I'm going to keep my eyes on the river as we move along. If any creature is going to pop its head out and stare at me, I want to see it first.

Aboard Namaab Again

Abram and Sarai want us to hurry, so I've decided

to try writing a little bit while riding on my sweet donkey. Dibri has agreed to ride with Gamilat for a time. They are becoming the best of friends! Namaah needs very little assistance from me now. She knows to follow the others, and I hardly ever have to give her direction.

I've bunched up a cloak in front of me and set you, my little diary, on top. It's like a little table! Sometimes, though, the ride is a bit bumpy. If this looks messy, I'll remember why.

Sarai keeps telling me that it is good and important that I record everything about my journey. She thinks I'm so smart to be able to write. Pigat and Gamilat cannot write, but I've promised to teach them someday. I guess I am recording this story for all of us then.

Pigat has pointed out so many wonders in the fields on our left. Of course, I recognize, the orange groves and fig trees. We had those in Haran. But I didn't know what the other greenery was here.

"Parsley, over there," Pigat pointed out, "and beyond there is mustard and wheat." She smiled at me. "I used to pull the weeds between the rows," she confided.

I'm marveling at the amount of food everywhere. It'll be impossible to go hungry here.

Pigat must've read my mind. "It'll flood soon," she said to no one in particular.

"What do you mean?" Gamilat asked.

"At the same time each year, the Nile floods its banks," Pigat said. "The pharaohs believe they have magical powers and they can control the floods. They appease the god of the Nile, Hapy, by leaving offerings on the riverbanks."

"That sounds terrible," I cried, "What about all the people who live close to the river?"

"They prepare for it," Pigat said matter-of-factly. "They watch the star Sirius. When it rises in the sky, they know that the Nile will flood. The flooding is a good thing, because the rich minerals that flow upriver are deposited into the fields. That's what makes the soil so good."

Sarai had been listening as she rode beside us. She motioned with her head toward the river. "The Nile is the lung of Egypt," she said. "If it weren't here, the people would die. Their entire lives revolve around this river. They honor it, revere it, and worship it, just like we honor, revere, and worship the one true God."

Yes, little diary: We—I—choose to worship the one true God.

From the Edge of the City

We're approaching a city built on the riverbanks. It's interesting! I've never seen anything like this before. I don't think Namaah has either, as she's stepping excitedly, making it more difficult to write just now.

Alongside us in the river, boats move in and out of the quay. Sailors unload jars of oil and wine. The city is enclosed in white walls of mud bricks. Outside its gates is a large open-air market.

As we move nearer the city, I pick up the smell of fresh bread. Oh, it smells delicious and calls us closer. I hear Sarai suggesting we should follow its fragrance into the market. We can't help ourselves. Other scents greet us at the market's edge. The smells of animals, spices, dusty grain, and overripe fruit mingle in the air. Sarai is ahead of me as I wait here and watch her move through the crowd.

The merchants crouch in little stalls. Sandals, pieces of cloth, breads, and cakes are spread out on low tables or hung from the roof. Chickens are in small pens, and fresh sardines wiggle in wet papyrus baskets. I'm so hungry my mouth is watering and my stomach aches—especially because I've spotted a stall with fresh guava, sycamore figs, garlic, and onions. Oh, and there are honeycombs glistening in the sun.

Those sailors in the quay sure make a lot of noise. They've walked off the boats with leather pouches slung over their shoulders. Now they're exchanging some of their rations of grain for fresh fruits and vegetables.

A moment ago there was a sudden flash of black fur. A monkey jumped up from a table! He clung to the leg of a man who was fleeing through the crowd. The merchant was pointing at him and yelling.

Sarai moved back and explained to me: "That man hasn't paid for the merchandise. The monkeys are trained to watch for these things and alert their people."

Abram was right. Every eye in Egypt, at least from the marketplace, does tend to follow Sarai. I feel nervous, so I'll stop making notes now. It's too hard anyway with all the people and commotion. I vow to keep my eyes on Sarai.

Oh, Why Did We Come Here?

I have only moments to write what is happening, and something tells me to make careful notes of it. I'm waiting with Sarai to be taken to Pharoah's palace. Yes, to Pharoah and the palace! We're in a dusty, narrow alley of the city, waiting for a flock of sheep on a city street to move out of the way.

Oh, will I ever see Javen and Dibri again?

Here's what happened, little diary, in case you are the one to tell all to my brothers. As we entered the market, we heard angry shouts from behind. I'd moved ahead to keep track of Sarai. She's my elder, but I sensed a need to protect her. My senses were right: When I heard the shouting, I turned to see two men pushing through the packed throng. They were staring at Sarai, walking in a straight line right toward us! I'd never seen men quite like these. They wore ankle-length kilts, leather sandals, and ornate necklaces on their otherwise bare chests.

Their heads were shaved.

Abram had caught up to us and was standing close. "Palace officials," he whispered to Sarai.

The men stepped in front of Abram. "Is this woman your wife?" they demanded. They gestured with their heads toward Sarai.

Sarai looked to Abram, but he wouldn't look at her. He stared at the ground.

"No, no," he mumbled. "She's my sister."

The men stepped closer to Sarai. "The Pharaoh requests your presence at once," they said.

Sarai clutched my hand. "I won't go anywhere without my companion Rhoda," she with urgency.

Javen and the others appeared behind Abram and Javen tried to take a step toward the officials. I could see the muscle in his cheek clench tight and quiver. Abram put a hand on his arm.

I moved slowly toward him and whispered, "I'll be back. I'm sure of it. They can't keep her. How can they?" Dibri, who had been walking with Gamilat, started to cry and my heart lurched. Quickly Gamilat scooped him up. He wrapped his arms around her neck and locked his hands together. Gamilat, trying to shift Dibri so she could see me better, was biting her lip.

At the last moment, Pigat ran up to me. "Just do what they say," she urged. "It'll be better for you that way."

Tears burned my eyes. We followed the two men through the crowd, my one hand clutching Sarai's tight fingers, and my other hand wrapped around you, my little diary. I turned to look back, but I could see no one. Abram and the others were lost in the noisy throng of people. We weaved our way through the merchant stalls. The white gates of the city swallowed us up. Dibri's mournful wails continued to ring in my ears long after they faded away—

Oh, Pharoah's men are motioning for us to get going again . . .

Where Am I?

I'm afraid! I feel very fuzzy about where I am and how I got here. Where's Sarai, or Pigat and Gamilat? I'm confused.

I was dragged from my sleep by the sound of trickling water. My eyes were so heavy; it was a great effort just to lift my lids. The room I'm in is dim and hazy, and the walls are very dark. I'm on some kind of a wooden bed covered in white cloth. Where is this place? How did I get here?

My head has been resting in a curved, wooden frame, and even sitting up, which took great effort, I feel heavy in every limb, from the top of my head to my toes. Why am I so tired and feeling so heavy?

Little diary, I found you here by my bed, and you are the only thing familiar to me.

Is this a dream?

What Time Is It?

It seems like a thick fog has wrapped itself around my head for days. It's just begun to lift, and I'm able to write more. I'll write as much as I can to help me think how I got here—to figure out where I am. There don't appear to be people walking around whom I can ask. Only people in beds, falling in and out of sleep or staring about, like me.

I was awakened again by the sound of trickling water. There are other sounds too. There's a deep groaning not far from me. My skin prickles and my heart races every time I hear such moans; they come from the people in other beds around me. They cry as if they are in pain. Every time I turn my head, I see more beds, more people who are stretched like I am. A golden statue is situated to the left of my bed. I've tried to push my head farther back to see it better, but I can only tell that it's a peculiar statue of a woman. A gold scorpion sits on top of her head.

To my right there's a small square of light that shines from the end of some sort of chamber. I've strained my eyes to see what's there. All I can make out is a man who appears to be pouring water over a tall statue.

Perhaps this is the trickling water that awakened me.

I see now that an animal skin is slung over the man's shoulders; the legs and the tail are still attached to the hide. The man looks equally strange. He has feathers dangling from his neck, and his head is bare and shiny.

I must rest myself again and think.

How do I know that strange man? Do I know him? Yes, he seems familiar to me. But where could

I have seen him?

Ah . . . I have a sudden, vague recollection. Did I dream of him? In my dream he stood at the foot of my bed and dangled a charm over my bandaged foot. He recited a verse in a tongue I don't know, and then he ladled water into my mouth like he does for that statue.

Wait! I can't believe what's happening! My foot felt so tight and sore, and when I looked down at it, I saw that it was indeed bandaged in a heavy, white gauze! Oh! Was my dream not a dream after all! Did this man bandage my foot? I can't even wiggle my toes. Little daggers of pain stab my foot when I try.

What has happened to me?

Without thinking, I've just reached up and felt for my charm. At least it's still there. I hold it in my left hand while I write in you, little diary, with my right hand. You're my only friends now. I'm in a strange place, and I have no idea how I got here. Even though I'm too big to cry, I'm very close to it.

I'm Growing (Dore Confused

I'm scared. I've pulled the sheet over me and up to my chin so I can write under the covers and appear as still as possible.

The last thing I remember is being in the marketplace with Sarai and having Pharoah's men tell us to follow them. We waited in the narrow street while one of the officials disappeared for a while. Then? What then? Oh! It's beginning to come back to me! I remember there was a sudden stab of pain in the bottom of my foot. Not like the pain now, but something worse, much worse. That pain shot up my leg, and I lost my balance. I remember Sarai catching my arm.

Then this place with the trickling water, the dreams that are not dreams . . . .

How long have I been here, and where is here? I still don't know. I must inhale deeply. This room is damp, and the air is stale and musty. There's another odor, an unpleasant one that I can't place.

Is this the palace?

This isn't what I imagined a king's palace would look like. It seems more like a dungeon.

I recall Pigat telling me as we moved along the

Nile that the cities and the palaces of Egypt are built on the east side of the river. What was that strange thing she said? Oh, yes: "This is where the sun rises and life begins."

Then Pigat pointed to the huge pyramids across the river. "Those are the temple complexes," she said. "They're the tombs and sacred buildings that honor the dead or dying. They're built on the west side of the Nile, where the sun sets and life ends."

My heart is racing now. I am beginning to tremble. Is that where I am—in the temple complex of the great pyramids?

I look around me again. Clay bowls with burning wicks sit on little tables. They smoke and give off a strong odor. Maybe that's the source of the unpleasant smell. The flame gives an amber glow and casts shadows on the walls. I shudder and close my eyes. Have I been buried in a tomb with these other people? Have we been left to die?

No, please, this can't be a tomb. There's light at the end of the chamber. I see trees and flowers beyond it now. But wait . . . it's the man with the animal skin on his shoulders . . .

He appeared in the doorway but has disappeared again. Should I could call to him? No, I'm too afraid . . . and maybe this really is a dream. Maybe in my dream I am having dreams. It's too hard for me to concentrate now. My thoughts are slipping further and further away . . .

Later

What a relief! I know now I'm in the sanatoria, which is a sort of Egyptian hospital. Sarai is here too! Well, not in the sanatoria, but nearby. She has visited me.

I must have fallen asleep after writing earlier. Here's what has happened: I awoke to a light but steady pressure on my arm, and then it was gone. I was hesitant to open my eyes. Was it the man again? I didn't want to know. Then there it was again.

"Dear Lord, please make her well," a familiar voice whispered.

My eyes flew open, and I saw Sarai standing beside me! Her hand was resting on my arm, and her eyes were wet and shiny and filled with worry.

I struggled to sit up, and Sarai helped me. I took her hand and held it in mine. "What happened?" I asked her. "Where am I?" I looked around again. "Is this a tomb?" My eyes began to water.

Sarai shook her head. She reached over and stroked my hair. "No, no. You're in the temple complex," she explained, "but it isn't a tomb. It's called the sanatoria."

She could see that I didn't understand.

"Let me tell you what happened," she said. "You'll feel better once you know. You collapsed before we ever reached the palace." She pointed to my bandaged foot. "You had a small hole in your sandal, and you stepped on an Egyptian scorpion"

A scorpion! That was the reason for the sudden pain in my foot!

"In addition," Sarai said, "you were already sick. Your body was nearly depleted of water. They carried you across the river and brought you here. It's where the sick or injured come when they want to be healed by the gods." She looked sad. "Their gods."

I sighed. "I'm not dying?" I asked her.

"No," Sarai told me. "God didn't let you die, but you could have. The sting of the Egyptian scorpion can be fatal. You drifted in and out of a deep,

deep sleep for at least seven or eight days."

I looked toward the square of light and saw the man again. "Who is he?" I asked. "I think he took care of me."

"Yes," Sarai said, nodding. "He did. He's one of the temple priests. He seeks the help and wisdom of his gods to treat the ill." She moved my hair away and whispered in my ear. "They believe their gods healed you, but we know better." She winked at me and smiled.

"He pours water on a statue out there," I told her. "I awakened every morning to the sound of trickling water."

"Those are statues of gods, which they believe have healing powers," Sarai told me. "The Egyptians pour water over the statues so their healing powers will pass into the water. Then they bathe the ill in this 'magic' water, or they have them drink it."

"Yes!" I cried. "I thought I remembered him ladling water into my mouth. I wasn't sure if it was a dream."

I pointed to the statue by my head. "Who's that?"

Sarai studied the golden figure. "I'm not so familiar with the Egyptian gods," she said, "but I believe, by the scorpion on her head, it's a statue of Selket, who the Egyptians believe is the goddess of magic, whose powers can cure the bite of a scorpion."

I shivered. I didn't like this place, and I definitely didn't like this statue by my head.

Sarai gently took my chin in her hands. "God is watching over you, Rhoda," she said. "You remember that. Still, we have to get you out of here. I'll bring you back to the palace, and you'll finish your recovery there."

I studied her for the first time. Something was very different. Her shawl was gone from around her head. Her hair was shorter, and it fell to her shoulders in a smooth, sleek line. A white robe covered one of her shoulders, and clung snugly to her body.

She looked beautiful, but I sensed she was unhappy.

"Sarai . . . ," I said, but I didn't know how to comfort her like she had just comforted me.

"Don't worry, Rhoda," Sarai said. "There will

be time for us to talk. I have much to tell you." She smiled, but her eyes looked sad.

"For now, you rest. I must go, but I'll be back and will bring you with me."

So, little diary, I'll do as Sarai says. I'll rest now.

I'm Leaving the Sanatoria . . .

Sarai has come for me, and we are sitting in a raft on the great river, waiting to cross to the other side. There are many boats, and we must wait until the river clears before we can make our short crossing.

Earlier, Sarai led me through the palace to a dark passageway. A servant was waiting for us. His dress was similar to that of the officials in the marketplace, with a long kilt, a bare chest, and a shaven head. He wasn't wearing a necklace though, and his feet were free of sandals.

The enormous temple rose behind us as we walked to the river. I'd never felt so relieved to leave anywhere as I felt about that temple. I squeezed Sarai's hand as I limped on my tender, bandaged foot.

We walked down the soggy slope of the river-bank and climbed into a papyrus raft. Another servant was waiting by it. Sarai and I sat on a woven reed mat—

Oh! It looks like we will be leaving. Two men have climbed onto our raft and are pushing, heavy oars through the gray, murky water as we begin our crossing.

"I should never have let you come," Sarai said to me a short while ago as we settled onto our mats. "It was wrong. I was very selfish."

I thought back to that day we were ordered to the palace. I didn't think it was Sarai who was selfish! I was still troubled by Abram's actions.

"I would've come anyway," I told Sarai. "Someone had to watch out for you."

Sarai laughed her beautiful laugh. It was music to me. I hadn't heard that laugh for a long, long time.

I just looked over the side of the raft and saw a long, green water snake slither to the surface then disappear. Blue and white lotus blossoms peek out from the floating lily pads. I remember Pigat telling me that the blue lilies open at daybreak with the morning sun, and the white lilies spread their petals at dusk.

I can see Pharoah's palace. It looms huge on the riverbank. Even from here I can see how the enormous columns rise above the white walls of the city. To Egyptians it may be beautiful, but not to me. I'd rather be in a tent in the Negev with Sarai and Abram and . . .

Oh, how I miss Dibri and Javen. I even miss Pigat and Gamilat. They're more than friends now. They're my family.

Does Sarai miss Abram after all he's done?

I look over at her. She was quiet for a long while, but now she suddenly seems talkative again.

Still Crossing the River

Sarai just told me something startling. It seems that as soon as she and I arrived at the palace, the pharaoh and his household were besieged with plagues.

Pharoah believes that we have our gods, just like he has his gods, Sarai explained. She said Pharoah was worried that her presence in the palace had angered our God.

"Has it?" I asked.

"Rhoda," Sarai said, leaning toward me. "God is not pleased that I am here. I should not be here. We should not be here. But, he has his mighty hand on both of us. I know this."

I must've looked doubtful.

"I haven't been called to Pharaoh's chambers yet," she whispered. "Every woman who enters the harem must be purified before she's permitted to see the king, but I believe it's not just Egyptian law that has kept me from being called to the king."

We had reached the other side of the river. The boat bumped gently into the soft, muddy bank, and. servants waiting to unload crates extended their hands and helped us out of the rafts. I have just a few more minutes to write.

Sarai just pointed to a narrow maze of streets leading to the eastern face of the huge palace.

Look!" she gasped.

Even from here I can see a terrace of eight towering columns, four of which stood on either side of a large window.

"Every morning before daybreak, Pharaoh's

subjects gather below the window and wait," Sarai said. "As the sun's rays peek over the broad horizon, Pharaoh climbs a hidden staircase. He appears in the window as the rising sun."

The Egyptian Harem Is Amazing

It's more luxurious than anything I could've imagined. The carved wooden chairs have ivory legs made to look like bulls' hooves or lions' paws. There are collapsible stools with leather seats and long couches with cushions. The walls are decorated with painted frescoes, and the tiled floor is etched with lotus blossoms. Large storage chests with rounded lids are made from alabaster.

I was relieved and embarrassed to be served a glorious meal upon our arrival. Sarai ate with me. She laughed at my appetite, but it's been such a long time since I've sunk my teeth into anything but bread and figs.

"One thing about the pharoah," Sarai whispered, laughing: "He knows how to provide a good meal."

Indeed! There was crispy roasted fish with fragrant garlic bulbs, onions, boiled cabbage, leeks, lentils, and radishes. There were also lettuce leaves, which the Egyptians dip into olive oil and salt and eat whole. There were also sweet lotus roots and then tasty bread made from the lotus plant.

After that feast, a strange thing occurred. I was measured and bathed. Measured! I'm unaccustomed to all this fussing and primping, but my words fall on deaf ears. The servants don't understand me, nor I them. They just look at me and laugh.

I didn't laugh when my body and teeth were scrubbed with a white paste that contained myrrh. I was smothered with oils and creams mixed with chalk. It seemed like a lot of fuss, and I missed our simple baths in the rivers. Then I ran my hand over my arm in disbelief. My skin has always been dry and chafed. It's silky soft now.

Pharoah's servants then dressed me in a white linen sheath similar to Sarai's. They lifted a necklace of glass beads over my head. I couldn't stop rubbing them with my fingers. The baubles were red, blue, and yellow, and they reflected the sun streaming in through the high, tiny windows.

I was so entranced by the colorful glass that I paid no attention as they whirled around me with bowls and brushes and beauty treatments.

I did notice some beautiful boxes stacked in one corner. A servant picked one out and brought it to me. She pulled out slinky black hair and slid it over my head. It was thick and even and fell to my shoulders. A straight fringe of bangs decorated my forehead. It looked just like Sarai's new hairdo, and it was only then that I realized Sarai must be wearing this false hair too! I looked at her, astonished.

Sarai broke into laughter. She brought a square of polished copper to me and held it in front of my face.

"Look at you, Rhoda!" she exclaimed. "You're breathtaking! If we don't get you out of here fast, a fine Egyptian boy will surely try to catch your eye."

She laughed even harder as I peeked into the mirror and jumped! There was green paint on my eyes, my cheeks were stained red, and my lips were painted bluish black. With my new fringe of black bangs, I didn't recognize myself. I was used to my mussed up hair and my pale eyes and lips. I didn't think I liked this new, exotic creature staring back at me.

Something brushed against my leg just then,

and I looked down to see another creature—a sleek, gray cat. It had very short ears, a lean body, and long legs. A shiny pendant hung from its neck. The pendant was a figure etched in silver, with the body of a woman and the head of a cat.

Most Egyptians, I noticed, wore pendants like these. The priest in the sanatoria had held something similar over my foot. I'd seen one servant wearing a pendant in the shape of a crocodile and another servant wearing a charm carved like a hippopotamus. I was surprised to see one on a cat, though. I asked Sarai about these charms and necklaces.

"They're called amulets," she said. "The Egyptians believe these charms possess magical powers and these powers are passed on to whoever wears them." She touched the charm from Mama around my own neck. "Do you think yours has magical powers?" she asked.

"I used to," I said, "but I don't anymore. This one belonged to Mama."

I pointed to the crescent moon.

"Yes, "Sarai said, "I recognize it—the symbol of Nanna, the moon goddess."

A wave of exhaustion and sadness washed over me. I looked around the room. Everything was so beautiful here, but I didn't care a thing about it. I missed the tent and the smell of dust and sand in the air. I missed Naamah's warm, sturdy back when she carried me. I even missed Dibri's body slumped across my lap. I missed the smell of the earth and the scent of the breeze as I laid my head down at night.

Here I couldn't see the stars or hear the lonely cries of the desert jackals as they called to one another. Suddenly, my face and head were hot and itchy from the wig and face paint. For the second time, the sleek cat rubbed against my leg. I was sure its pendant was glowing in the dimming light of the harem. Curiosity distracted me from discomfort.

"Why does the cat wear a charm?" I asked Sarai.

She crouched down and stroked the cat's head while she examined the amulet. "This is the drawing of a goddess. It may be that the Egyptians believe this goddess protects cats. Amulets are also worn for protection." She pointed to one on the neck of a young servant. It was gold and in the shape of a frog. "The frog is a symbol of fertility," Sarai pointed out. "She wears it to ensure that her womb will give life to many children someday."

Sarai grew pensive then.

"It's a good time to sleep," she said.

I climbed into my bed and settled my head in the strange wooden headrest—just like the one at the sanatoria. Then I decided to write about this most odd day.

I wonder what Dibri and Javen are doing.

What a Surprising Day

A servant awakened Sarai and me before dawn. She returned our tunics, which had been washed and neatly folded. My old, worn sandals had been re-placed with new Egyptian ones. They were tied with two thongs and had a pointed tip that turned upwards. I liked them very much and smiled broadly at the girl who gave them to me. My heart beat fast with anticipation.

"What does this mean?" I asked Sarai. I didn't want to get up my hopes.

Sarai looked at the young servant. She pointed toward herself and then toward the window. The girl nodded. I did the same thing; I wanted to make sure. The girl laughed and nodded again.

"Pharaoh must have decided it was in his best interests to let us go," Sarai said. She laughed and grabbed my hands to whirl me around the room. "Pharoah may not worship our God, but he fears him. If plagues have struck his household, he's smart enough to know God brought them upon him. Even if Pharaoh didn't know I was married when I came here, God did."

We quickly changed into our old tunics and folded our linen sheaths to leave on the beds. I had already taken off my false hair and my glass jewels before I went to sleep. Sarai had done the same.

The officials who'd led us to the palace were waiting for us outside the harem. Once again they led us through the marketplace, only this time I was careful to watch for scorpions!

The crowd seemed thicker today, and several times we lost sight of the officials altogether. Then I spotted Dibri's tiny figure. His brown hair was tousled, and he was holding Javen's hand.

Abram stood beside them.

When Dibri saw me, he pointed and tugged on Javen's arm. Javen nodded, and Dibri ran at full speed to jump into my arms. I buried my head in his hair, which smelled like dust. I loved it.

Javen brought Naamah to me. Then he put his arm around my shoulders and squeezed me close. Frowning, he shook his head when he saw my Egyptian makeup. Some of it had rubbed off when I slept, but there were still smudges of green around my eyes.

"What did they do to you?" he asked. "Are you all right?"

"Yes, Javen," I told him. "I'm fine. They were very gracious. They took care of me, but I'm glad to be with you again. I have a lot to tell."

Javen boosted me onto Naamah's back. How I'd missed my sweet donkey. I stroked her soft head and thought it seemed like she was smiling at me with her big, sweet eyes. Dibri wouldn't leave me. He sat in front and pressed against me as tightly as he could.

Sarai rode ahead, and Abram walked beside her. When I saw them together, I was troubled again.

"Javen?" I said.

He stared straight ahead, but I could see that he was smiling. "I was counting," he said.

"Counting?" I repeated.

"Yes," he said. "I was counting how long it'd take for you to ask me."

I thought about this for a moment.

"Well?" he said.

This conversation was very strange. Did he know me that well? "All right then," I said. "Why did Abram lie about Sarai?"

My big brother twisted his mouth to one side and chewed on his lip. He had a sparse beard, and it looked like he'd make it more sparse by the way he rubbed it with his fingers. I was reminded of Papa.

"Why do you think he lied?" Javen returned my question with a question. He was becoming more like Papa than I imagined!

I hesitated a few moments before answering. "I think Abram was afraid," I slowly admitted. I could see a large cluster of tents ahead, but I knew they weren't Abram's. There were far too many.

Javen stopped and took hold of Naamah. He stood in front of her so he could look into my face.

"Look," Javen said. His tone was serious, but I sensed a deep love coming from him. "It's not easy to believe in a God we can't see. Why do you think people make idols and worship them?"

I had no reply.

Javen didn't wait long for one either.

"It's because it's easier to believe in something you can see and touch," he said. "People turn back to idols when they think God doesn't see them or care about them."

"But idols aren't real," I protested. "That's why Papa told me the story about Abram. Besides, Abram doesn't believe in idols anyhow, remember? He realized that even if you can see them and touch them, idols can't do anything. They have no power. So how could they be gods?"

Javen was laughing now. "Rhoda," he said. "I agree with you. I'm just reminding you that it takes practice to perfect our faith. It's easy to believe in something you can see. Anybody can do that. But we have faith because we believe in something we've never seen."

He touched my pendant. "Whether you admit it or not, you wear this pendant because it makes you feel safe. That's what Mama taught you, and you're not quite ready to believe that God can and will protect you. Otherwise, you'd be done with this. So what's the difference between your lack of faith and Abram's?"

I looked down at the necklace from Mama and sighed. Javen was right, as usual. I did believe in Abram and Sarai's God, but even in the sanatoria I'd held on to this charm. I've told myself that I wear it because it reminds me of Mama. In my heart I know that's not the only reason.

Maybe I've judged Abram too harshly. Maybe we're not so different.

Later

It's so good to be with our household again and resting now in my own camp. I hadn't realized earlier that Javen was leading me toward the huge camp I'd thought belonged to someone else. There were hundreds of animals grazing nearby. It wasn't until Gamilat and Pigat ran up that I realized this was our camp.

The flocks were at least ten times larger than when Sarai and I were taken from everyone. And there were camels! Lots and lots of camels, loads of oxen, and many more sheep and donkeys. Servants walked here, there, and everywhere.

Abram and Sarai's household had grown to the size of a little city.

Gamilat reached me first and gently pulled me from Naamah. Had I been away so long? She looked different to me. Her hair was neater than usual, tied back with a scarf. I could see the red highlights from the wisps that peeked out from her scarf.

Javen cleared his throat. He walked a few steps, then turned back and looked at us before moving on again. Gamilat stared after him. When she swung her head toward me, I noticed that she was blushing.

She saw me watching her and quickly tried to help Dibri down. He couldn't be pried loose. He squeezed my hand with his white knuckles, and with his other arm he clutched my leg.

Gamilat laughed at him. "What about me?" she teased him. "You were my friend when your sister was gone. Now that she's returned, you'll just forget about me?"

It was no use. Dibri squeezed me tighter. His fingers were like talons and dug into my flesh. I reached down and kissed his hair. "It's all right," I whispered. "You can stay with me."

Pigat had reached us. Her eyes were wise, just as Gamilat's were whimsical. She hugged me, then spread out her arm toward the camp.

"What happened?" I asked her. "Where did all this come from?"

"From Pharaoh," she said. "Some of it was given to Abram after you and Sarai left. Some of it was given just yesterday—"

"You haven't told us what happened," interrupted Gamilat. "But I can see by your face that you were treated well."

"You look silly," said Dibri. He pulled me down and studied my face. "What's on your eyes? Is it dirt?"

I tickled him until the tears ran down his dirty cheeks like a river running through the sand.

We are to leave Egypt in the morning. Already the camp is in disarray. The mens' tents are being torn down, and poles and ropes litter the ground. It's a wonderful sight as far as I'm concerned. I'm tired and hungry, but I'm happy. I'm home!

We Leave after Dawn

I was engrossed in my morning tasks when I heard a sudden bellow behind me. I jumped and heard Dibri and Javen's laughter. I turned to see three enormous camels. Dibri was sitting on the largest of the three.

Javen bowed low. "I would like to introduce you to your camels," he said. "They will accompany you on your journey back to Canaan."

Gamilat, standing nearby, laughed. I watched her eyeing Javen. I thought I'd noticed something yesterday, and now I was sure of it. Javen had never been so playful, and Gamilat's cheeks were flushed every time she was near him. Pigat looked at me and smirked.

I looked at the camels again and thought of Naamah. Why couldn't I ride my sweet little donkey? Javen told me the camels were better suited for long treks in the desert. He said it was a burden for Naamah to carry heavy loads in such extreme conditions. On our return trek to Canaan, it would be hotter than before.

"I've never ridden a camel before, Javen," I reminded him. "They're awfully big."

"Ride with me," Dibri called. "Ride with me."

I walked over to him and looked up. "How did you get up there anyway?"

Dibri laughed.

"Yell *bejao!*" Javen urged.

Without warning the camel lurched forward and dropped to his knees, tucking his front legs beneath him. His back legs collapsed then, and he shuffled until his breastbone dropped to the ground.

Dibri couldn't stop giggling. "See?"

We're Returning to Canaan

We left Egypt that morning under the watchful eye of the towering temples. A convoy of Egyptian soldiers on horseback accompanied us out of the country. Our caravan was long and moved slowly.

It took me a few days to get used to riding on my camel. I was expecting a ride similar to that of Naamah, but I was mistaken. Traveling on a camel is very complicated. Once I mastered the command *bejao*, I could get any camel to crouch anywhere. I climbed on a rolled-up blanket behind the camel's hump and squeezed Dibri in front of me. I held the ropes attached to its nose pegs and patiently waited for the camel to get up. It didn't budge.

Dibri shook his head in exasperation. *"Utho!"* he shouted. "Hang on!" The camel straightened its hind legs first, which propelled us forward with a jerk. Only when we were hanging forward, squished against its hard hump, did it decide to straighten its front legs and lift us to dizzying heights off the ground.

"Now say *Jaldi! Jaldi!*" Dibri whispered with a gleam in his eyes.

I didn't trust him. He looked like he was up to some game. "What does that mean?" I asked him with narrowed eyes. "What language is this, anyway? And for that matter, how do you know all of this?"

"They taught me," he said with a shrug toward some of the servants. "The camels are from India, so this is how they talk."

Dibri pulled me down and cupped my ear with his chubby fingers. I felt his warm breath on my cheek. *"Jaldi* means 'move,'" he whispered. "If I say it too loud, they'll hear me and move."

We've been "moving" on these camels for many

days now, and I'm doing much better. When camels walk, they sway from side to side. Both the front and back legs of the left side move forward at the same time, and then the right legs move. The pads in their feet spread when they walk to keep their feet from sinking into the sand.

Javen said camels are the "ships of the desert." I suppose it isn't surprising, then, that I've been sick to my stomach for the last few days.

Now Back to Bethel

It's been twenty days since we left Egypt. Our return trip was slow, not only because there were more of us, but also because the land to the north was at a much higher elevation. We climbed and climbed and climbed before making a camp in the same forested hills where we'd settled before we left for Egypt.

This time Abram has chosen the topmost summit to set up camp. There's a huge grove of olive trees, which will provide wonderful shade for our tents. We can also see for miles in every direction.

Things aren't the same as before we went to

Egypt, and I'm sad about it. Our household has grown so large. We're no longer a cozy little family. There are more faces I don't know and some faces I only recognize in passing—enough for only a greeting. I'm grateful that Pigat and Gamilat still share my tent. We're close like sisters.

Gamilat disappears for longer periods of time now. She often volunteers to bring lunch to the shepherds in the pastureland. Dibri helps her carry the bundles of food. Pigat and I both know it's because of Javen. Thanks to my unsuspecting spy, little Dibri, I'm able to glean information.

"What does Gamilat do in the pasture after she has delivered the lunches?" I asked him one day.

"She talks to Javen," Dibri said. "They talk a lot."

I'm very happy about it. I love Javen, and I adore Gamilat. Papa isn't here to help Javen find a suitable wife, so it couldn't have worked out better. Gamilat seems to make him very happy, and I know she's a wonderful person.

I see Sarai every day. She seeks me out more, but we don't talk much. In fact, she's been very quiet lately. Perhaps she's tired from the journey.

A Parting of Ways ~ Hebron

Gamilat rushed into the tent this morning. She'd disappeared just after dawn. I was sweeping out the dust, and Pigat was rolling up the sides.

"Something's happening with the herdsmen!" she cried. "It's not good."

"What?" I asked her. "Is it Javen? Is something wrong?"

"No, Javen is fine," she said, "but he continually tries to settle disputes between Abram's herdsmen and Lot's. There are too many herds now and not enough land. They fight over the grazing areas and the water."

Gamilat was right. Later that day, we overheard Abram and Lot on the outskirts of camp. They stood on the edge of the hill.

"I don't want there to be any quarreling between you and me," Abram told him. It was windy. Their tunics were pressed against their bodies, and their voices carried across the camp. "Nor do I want our herdsmen to quarrel with one another. We're family."

I saw Lot nod his head in agreement. Abram put one arm around his nephew's shoulders, and he stretched out the other in front of him. "The whole land is spread out before you. Let's part company. If you go to the left, I will go to the right. If you go to the right, I will go to the left."

To the east is the Jordan River and the broad, green meadows on either bank. Little streams cut through the plain. I saw Lot point to the east, and Abram nodded his head. He reached down, took off his sandal and handed it to his nephew. He had sealed the agreement.

The next morning, we packed up our camp again. I found Sarai alone. "Where will we go?" I asked her. "Lot has chosen the best land."

"We'll go to the west," she said. "There are valleys that are livable. Rhoda, Lot lacks wisdom. The land to the east is fertile, yes, but he hasn't considered the people who inhabit that same land. They're a wicked, sinful group of men and women. He'll have to live among them."

So that's why we move from place to place like true nomads these days. We're in this camp just for tonight, then tomorrow we'll pack up again, travel on to another spot, pitch our tents, then pull up the stakes again.

A New Home

It's dark, but the stars shine brightly tonight. I love to lie on my mat in the cool of night, right under the stars. How different from when we first began traveling as a household so long ago.

These stars are winking down on what I think will be our new home. We came upon this place late today, but nightfall was coming and it was too late to pitch our tents, so we're all in the open air tonight.

It has a delicious smell, of earth and . . . is that the sea?

We're not far from the Salt Sea, Sarai tells me. We're sunk in a valley, like Sarai spoke of, surrounded by hills bearing huge wild grapes.

How grateful I am to know we'll settle here for a while.

Sarai seems grateful too. She laughed as she helped us unpack our mats and get ready for sleep.

As for Abram, he must be most grateful. He's gone off to make an altar to God, lit by the moon as he walked peacefully into the shadows.

Papers Stuck Inside Diary One
More than Ten Years Later

2080 B.C.

Our Household

I'm seventeen now, and our household has grown.
Now we have with us . . . .

Javen: My brother is twenty-five now, and married to Gamilat.
Gamilat: My sister-in-law is twenty-two.
Azaz: My nephew, Javen and Gamilat's son, is seven.
Phoebe: My precocious niece, Javen and Gamilat's daughter, is five.
Dibri: Our baby brother is growing into a young man, fifteen!
Abram: He's the head of everything, and is eighty-six.
Sarai: She's like a mother to me. She's seventy-six.
Pigat: At twenty-one, she's become an old friend.
Jairus: Pigat's husband is twenty-nine.

Julia: Pigat and Jairus's daughter is five years old.

Hebron

How long it's been since I've confided in a diary. Sarai says there are seasons in every girl's, and woman's, life. The last decade must've been my busy season. Since I filled this little diary, I've been busy helping Sarai and Abram and our household make a home.

I feel the tug these days, though, to sort out my thoughts more.

How my first diary helped me do that! I look back on those days by reading the entries on the pages I sewed together with woven threads of strong papyrus grass.

I think a lot these days about that time when Javen and Dibri and I came to live with Abram and Sarai. Things seemed simpler then. I had to worry only about Dibri and myself, and helping Sarai. Javen took care of himself, and, I am loathe to admit, of Dibri and me—more than I understood then.

We are such a large household now. My friends have married and have children, and so I take care of Pigat and Jarius's little daughter, Julia, a squirmy five-year-old with more energy than me, at least most of the time.

How our household continues to grow! Just this morning Gamilat gave birth to another little boy. That makes three children for her and Javen. Her body is very tired though, and this birth was quite difficult. I told her she should stop at three. It's a good number.

Javen paced back and forth outside the birth tent. For hours he listened to Gamilat's moans. When I walked out with his new baby, he was sitting on the ground with his face in his hands.

"Javen!" I called softly so as not to startle him. I held out the little bundle wrapped in cloth. "You have another son."

Tears dropped from his red eyes, and he reached for the baby as if it were a fragile egg. He was exhausted too.

"It never gets any easier, Rhoda," he told me. "It's pure torture as I listen to her pain. I still think of Mama, and I'm filled with fear that Gamilat will die in childbirth like she did."

His face was creased with worry.

I put my arms around him and the baby. We'd grown so close, and we'd come such a long way in the last ten years.

"I know, Javen," I told him, "but look. Your new little one is fine. Gamilat is healthy and strong and just fine too." I hugged him. This is the last baby. I told her so."

Their oldest, Azaz, is strong and thoughtful, just like his father. He makes a fine shepherd already and helps Dibri and Javen in the pasture-land. Phoebe looks exactly like her mother. She even has the same mischievous twinkle in her eyes.

It's a blessing that Phoebe and Julia are the same age. I never dreamed that my friends' children would play together, but it's more than I could've hoped for. When Javen, Dibri, and I left Haran, we left behind all that was familiar to us. Now Abram and Sarai's household has become ours. We're woven together so tightly that I can't imagine my life without any of them.

Dibri is betrothed to a beautiful girl named Lois. She's so lovely, and Dibri reminds me so much of Papa. He's taller, though, and quite strik-ing. He's also a fine shepherd, just like his brother.

Sarai grows more distant with each new baby born into the household. She loves them all, but it's evident to everyone that she's unfulfilled. I don't blame her. She's watched so many in her household bear children at a young age. But she's seventy-six, and her womb is barren. I know God promised that she and Abram would have many offspring, but every year comes and every year goes. Still there's no sign of a child for them.

Sometimes I want to talk with Javen about this. "If God promised they'd have children, then they'll have children," he always says. That's all he'll say about it! He doesn't understand that sometimes I need to talk about it.

"Javen," I told him one night when we sat after dinner with Gamilat. "It's Sarai's greatest fear that she won't bear a child for her husband. It's every woman's greatest fear. Sarai lives with it every day of her life. She's slapped in the face each time a woman in our household gives life."

Gamilat looked at me knowingly. "Yes," she said. "Listen to Rhoda, Javen. She's saying a true thing."

Javen looked at us with a bit of surprise. He softened when he saw how sad we were. "But if we can't believe God to do the impossible, then he isn't God, is he?" Javen said after a long silence. He looked at me and nodded toward my necklace. "He's just an idol like the charm you still wear around your neck."

I sighed. "When will I stop hearing about this charm?" I asked him.

"When you take it off," he said. "Your mother lives in the blood that swims through your veins. She's part of you. You don't need a charm to remind you of her, and you don't need a charm to protect you either."

He smiled then. "You have God, and, of course, you have us."

It's Just Us Today

Javen, Dibri, and Jairus rose today at daybreak to lead the flocks farther away for good grazing. This means, of course, they may be gone for several days. I'm grateful for the company of Pigat and Gamilat during such lonely times. Though it gives me more of a chance to write in my diary, I'd get too lonely if all I did was spend time alone to write. I do love my girlfriends.

Pigat has brought me the most interesting news.

Her tent is the closest to Sarai's. At midmorning she rushed through my door and pulled me down. We sat cross-legged on the ground. "I overheard something," she said, trying to be quiet, though her voice was intense. "Can you talk?"

It was quiet, but I knew it wouldn't last long. All three of our girls were outside in the camp. Neri and Azaz had gone into the fields with the men. Gamilat and her baby were still recovering in the tent next to mine.

"Yes, yes," I told her. "Now is a good time. What did you hear?"

"Sarai asked Abram to take Hagar as his second wife," Pigat said. "Sarai said she'd thought about God's promise to give Abram many offspring, and because she's been barren all these years, she wants Hagar to have a baby for her."

Hagar! Tall, lanky Hagar with her black hair and skin the color of fig paste—Hagar, who keeps to herself and talks very little. Why would Sarai want this Egyptian slave to have a baby for her? Hagar is one of many handmaids given to Sarai and Abram by the pharaoh when we were in Egypt. Most of the Egyptian slaves in the household stay together. They don't mix with the others unless their duties require them to, but Hagar is especially reserved and dramatically distant.

"How can Hagar have one for her?" I asked Pigat.

"Slaves are the property of their mistresses or masters," Pigat explained. "Any child conceived by a slave in the household is the property of the household. So Hagar's child would belong to Sarai and Abram."

Was this how God intended to give Abram and Sarai a child? It didn't seem right.

As usual, Pigat seemed to read my thoughts.

"I think Sarai feels pressured," she said sadly. "Perhaps Ara's birth was the last straw. She saw Gamilat's joy, and I think she felt overjoyed too at Ara's beauty and sweetness. But that seemed to make her even more sad. You know how she yearns to have a baby but can't conceive. I see her spending less and less time with all the children, and I remember how she loved to take every moment she could to play with them and comfort them. Remember how she mothered us when were little?"

I remembered. I thought of the time in

Pharoah's palace when she sat by me at the sanatoria, and when we whirled round the room with joy, knowing we could go back to our own camp and people. All Sarai ever wanted was to make a loving home of peace and grace. She wanted to fill it with children and laughter.

Poor Sarai

I understand how she feels. When Gamilat had her first baby, I had an insatiable desire to have my own child. I thought about babies every minute of every day. They even cried in my dreams during the night.

The desire was irrepressible, and it still hasn't gone away.

That's one reason, I think, I crave time to put down my thoughts on paper again. I too want a husband and a child and a home. I dream of these things. But I'm young and have great hopes; Sarai has a husband and a home, but no children, and she's old.

I have thought about this for days, and I'm feeling more and more unsettled. Nothing feels right about these new events. I long to ask Sarai about this, but of course, none of us are supposed to know.

Sarai would be angry at Pigat for eavesdropping and then telling what she heard.

I fear trouble lurks at our door.

Hagar Has Conceived

All that Pigat heard has come to pass. Hagar's belly is ripe and swollen like a plump date. She struts about the camp and acts like she's the mistress of the household. She's insolent and rude toward Sarai because she knows she'll give Abram something Sarai never could: a baby.

We're all upset, but Pigat is like a mother hen. She's protective of Sarai and always has been. There was an eruption at dinner last night. The men were served their supper on a long leather cloth. Then the women sat down to eat their portion.

All, that is, except Hagar.

"What's this?" she spat. Her teeth were yellow and sharp, and she reminded me of a wild cat. "There's no meat again?" She narrowed her eyes and glared at Sarai.

"I bear the child who will inherit Abram's fortune and will carry on his name. I won't eat such simple food as this."

Pigat rose and stood threateningly close to Hagar. I could see Pigat's fists clenched behind her back. "Don't ever speak to Sarai that way again," she said finally, unclenching one fist and letting the anger seep into her words, which were deep, long, and drawn out in a low voice. "Sarai is the true mistress of the house. Your worth is but a fleck of dust that will be carried away as the soon as the wind blows—and it will blow."

I was shocked, as was Gamilat. We'd never heard Pigat speak a harsh word. In a way, we were proud of her. She echoed all of our sentiments.

Sarai didn't say a word to Hagar.

Instead, she stood with remarkable grace and poise. She walked to Abram. "You are responsible for the wrong I'm suffering." Her voice was eerily calm, but her eyes were like daggers. "May the Lord judge between you and me."

Her words seemed to echo in the silence. The women had stopped chewing their food, and in the background the men had hushed their after-dinner talk. Even the children were still. They sensed the tension and were confused by it. The littlest ones didn't understand at all and could only glance warily from Abram to Sarai with wide, fearful eyes.

I could hear Sarai's rapid breath and see her chest heave with indignation.

Abram sighed. He sat in silence with profound sadness in his eyes. Finally, he held up his hands and shook his head. "Sarai," he said quietly, though all of us could hear, "your servant is in your hands. Do with her whatever you think best."

Sarai flung around with a fury that surprised everyone, especially the insolent Hagar. Grabbing Hagar's arm, Sarai moved quickly away, behind a grove of trees. Hagar could only stumble along until she and Sarai were out of our sight.

Murmurs began among the women, but a moment later Hagar's cry caused a hush again.

In silence we watched Sarai walk steadily, head held high, to her tent. She appeared calm, but Pigat, Gamilat, and I could sense her frustration and sadness behind the sudden calm and poise.

As we cleaned up from supper, Hagar's wails faded into the night. None of us dared say a word.

Later

I've just come from sitting with Gamilat and Pigat, far from the others. All the children have been sent to bed. The men have gone separate ways, as have the servants and other women.

Gamilat, Pigat, and I needed the comfort of one another, though, after tonight's dinner scene with Hagar.

"I don't understand what happened," Pigat cried. "I couldn't help myself, my words."

"It wasn't you who started this," Gamilat soothed.

"I've never seen Sarai this way," I cried.

"Javen believes Sarai reacted in a foolish way," Gamilat said.

"Do you believe that?" I asked.

"I don't know," Gamilat said. She heaved a deep sigh. "Sarai doesn't believe God will do what he promised. She took matters into her own hands when she gave Hagar to Abram. Then, when her simple slave conceived the child she couldn't, it crushed her. She was jealous."

"But that's what she wanted," I said. "She wanted Hagar to bear Abram's child."

"She didn't really want that, Rhoda," Gamilat said. "Let's be honest. We're all women here. Sarai might have accepted the fact Hagar could bear Abram's child if Hagar hadn't exalted herself as she did. Hagar humiliated Sarai, privately certainly. Then tonight, in front of all of us, Hagar drove a dagger of words right into Sarai's womb with her insolence. Sarai's anger, though, may be more at Abram than Hagar."

"Yes, I suppose I can see that," I admitted.

Even though I wasn't fond of Hagar, I felt sorry for her. It was sundown, and she hadn't returned to the camp. She was alone in the night with a baby in her belly, with no husband to take care of her. It wasn't right.

"God," I prayed silently, "watch out for Hagar, wherever she is."

As usual Pigat must've read my thoughts and prayers. "Rhoda," she said, "Hagar did wrong when she ran away. She abandoned her mistress and her master. She provoked Sarai, then deserted her service."

"Yes," I replied, remembering Javen's words about Abram when Sarai and I had returned from the pharoah's palace. I repeated them. "But it takes practice to make ourselves perfect."

Pigat, Gamilat, and I stared up at the night sky in search of the stars we've watched together so many nights. But even the stars are hidden tonight, and the sky, like the mood throughout our household, is black.

Hagar Has Returned

She isn't flaunting her pregnancy anymore, but she and Sarai avoid one another as much as possible. None of us speak of the events at dinner yesterday, but they're on everyone's minds. Unspoken divisions are beginning in our household: There are those who feel more sorry for Sarai, and those who sympathize more with Hagar. Discontent has put all of us on edge, and I sorely miss Sarai's laughter.

The Baby Has Arrived

Just a few hours ago, Hagar gave birth to Abram's first son. Hagar told us God had already named him Ishmael, which means "God hears." She said God appeared to her as she sat crying beside a spring that evening when Sarai dragged her from the dinner table and she ran away.

Hagar said God told her she would have a son who would be like a wild donkey.

That's the most Hagar has ever spoken to us!

Anyway, if her son's birth is any indication of his temperament, then I know she tells the truth. Ishmael kicked and screamed his way out of her womb.

None of us have seen Sarai today. She's been in her tent all morning, and there's no sign that she'll show her face today.

Diary Two
A Time for Laughter

Thirteen Years Later ~

2067 B.C..–2066 B.C.

Household Tree

I'm thirty and just now starting my second diary!
How time has changed us:

Hori: My husband is thirty-five—yes, I'm married!
    Neri: Our son is now ten.
    Zara: Our daughter is nine.

Javen: My brother is thirty-eight now.
Gamilat: My sister-in-law is thirty-five.
    Azaz: Their son is twenty.
    Phoebe: Their oldest daughter is eighteen.
    Ara: The baby is no longer a baby, but thirteen.

Dibri: My brother has grown into an impressive man of twenty-eight.
Lois: His wife is twenty-six.
    Jael: Their oldest son is seven.
    Rhesa: Their oldest daughter is five.
    Jarib: My nephew is a rambunctious four-year-old.
    Janna: The baby girl is just two.

Abram: He still rules our household. He's ninety-nine.
Sarai: She's still beautiful at eighty-nine.
    Ishmael: Their son by Hagar is thirteen.

Pigat: At thirty-four, she's one of my longest-time friends.
Jairus: Her husband is forty-two.
Julia: Their daughter is eighteen.

Hebron

I came across my little diary the other day. I'd almost forgotten the joy that comes from recording the events of one's life, all the good and bad, happy and sad, in a secret place. When I found my last writings stuck on papers folded into the back of my old diary, I knew it was time to make a new one. So, my friend, you'll keep my secrets and thoughts, and maybe someday, when I'm dead and gone, you'll carry them to my children.

I think of these things more now that I'm a mother.

God has blessed me so with such a good husband, Hori, who is a shepherd like Javen and Dibri. God has also blessed me with children—as he has Pigat and Gamilat. We're all blessed, except Sarai. It's a mystery as to why she of all women hasn't been given children of her own.

Ishmael isn't the comfort she expected. Still, Sarai laughs through her disappointments. Her laugh isn't the carefree one I remember from childhood, but it's a way of coping, I think.

I've Seen This Before

Abram walked into the camp yesterday, and I was transfixed by his appearance. An aura seemed to radiate from him. It reminds me of the time years ago when he left our first camp to make an altar. When he returned, he possessed a similar luminescence.

This time seemed a little different though . . . more intense. When Abram passed, I felt a breeze that stirred me from within and made me weep.

Sarai stared at him from the entrance to her tent. She barely blinked as she watched him walk toward her. She saw something too. Abram went to her and fell down at her feet. Tears rolled down his cheeks and wetted his beard. He reached for her hands, and then he began to laugh. It began in his belly and moved through him until his entire body shook with raw emotion.

"Beloved wife," he cried, "the Lord has appeared to me this day. "He made a covenant with me!"

Sarai looked toward the oak where Abram had been.

"God said I will be the father of many nations. My name is no longer *Abram*, but *Abraham*," he told her. "You, Sarai, will be the mother of nations. Your name is now *Sarah*. This land of Canaan belongs to all of our descendants."

Sarah smirked and looked away. "So it is to Ishmael that this covenant will be given."

"No, Sarah," replied Abraham. "God will give you a child of your own, a boy called Isaac. God said he will bless Ishmael. He will make him fruitful and increase his numbers, but he will establish this covenant with Isaac only."

Sarah began to laugh then, just as Abram had. Her laughter poured out of her mouth, but it was much less like honey this time. It was laced with sheer shock, disbelief, and doubt. Then, as quickly as her laughter began, it died.

Zara, my daughter, had overheard and clutched my hand. "Mama," she said with sorrow. "Sarah doesn't think God will do this thing he promised."

"I know," I told her and nodded my head. "It's been so many years. Sarah has seen children like you born and grown. She sees her own body age and still mourns having no child of her own. She doesn't realize we're all her children in a way."

I watched a tear slip from the corner of Abraham's eye. Sarah caught it with her finger. She looked at him more tenderly than I had seen for a long time, then she bent down and kissed his cheek. "I'm nearly ninety years old, and you are nearly one hundred," she laughed softly, "and you are trying to tell me that God will give us a child now?"

"Yes, Sarah." His voice was thick with emotion. "This is indeed what God has revealed to me."

Later

Abraham has gathered all of the boys and men in the camp over the age of eight days. He circumcised himself, then circumcised each one of them. Sarah told Abraham to use the birth tent, and we stood outside to help nurse the men, and especially the boys.

Some of the women were upset, but Sarah explained that God told Abraham to circumcise all of the males as an everlasting sign of his covenant with him. So we watched proud men walk in with confidence, then hobble back out with humility.

Last night a chorus of male groans pierced the night and awakened every living creature in the land of Canaan. The wolves and the jackals commiserated with them. They lifted their noses to the full moon and howled until the sun broke over the horizon.

A Momentous Day

It didn't start out that way. It seemed this morning I'd never felt the air so still and so heavy. It clung to our skin like a warm, wet blanket. By the heat of the day, the air was especially sultry. There was little activity in the camp.

I sat this morning with Zara, Pigat, and Gamilat beneath a tree. The side of a tent was stretched over our laps, and we worked with fury to patch the holes with fresh pieces of goat-hair cloth. Our bone needles wove the goat-hair thread up and under in small, slanted stitches. We'd done this so many times throughout the years that our nimble fingers worked without heed to our brains.

The unusual heat, though, sapped our bodies of their energy. Even the small movement of our hands was tiresome. Droplets of perspiration fell onto the cloth.

"Look!" Zara said suddenly and pointed toward

the horizon. I'd been daydreaming and hadn't even noticed that she was on her feet. Three figures walked with purpose toward the camp. As they neared, we saw that they were men.

"How odd," remarked Pigat. She strained her eyes to see them better. "They walk on foot. The nearest camp is at least a three-day journey."

"It's not just that," Gamilat said. She stood to see them better, then frowned. "Strange," she muttered. "They carry no provisions. Not a water skin slung over their shoulders, not a walking stick, not a pouch or a bag of any sort."

We dropped our needles, and all of us stood. We watched the men move closer. They were very tall and broadly built, and it was evident they were intent upon approaching our camp. Abraham sat in the entrance of his tent, and when he spotted the three men he ran to greet them.

I thought back to my first experience with the Bedouins and how amazed I was at their gracious generosity. I've since learned that Abraham and all nomads, for that matter, live and die by this strict code of hospitality.

"Who are they?" asked Zara. "Did you see

Abraham run to them? They must be important."

She was right. If the traveler was an ordinary person, Abraham would rise to his feet but never run toward them.

I shook my head. "I don't know, but there's something unusual about them." I was compelled to watch them for reasons I didn't understand.

Abraham bent down and bowed very low to the dirt. "If I've found favor in your eyes, Lord, do not pass your servant by. Let a little water be brought so you can wash the dust from your feet. Then, please rest under this tree."

Abraham lifted his head just a little. "Let me get you something to eat, so you can be refreshed and then go on your way."

"Very well," the men answered together. "Do as you say."

Abraham rose and led them to the grove of trees beside his tent. While they washed their feet with bowls of water, he left and returned with a calf. Pigat rushed forward and helped Sarah roast the meat over the fire. Then she served the bread Sarah baked with boiled wheat swimming in butter and melted fat.

They dipped their meat and bread into the juices before they ate, and Abraham leaned against the trunk of the widest tree and watched his guests with satisfaction. Pigat brought out cups of camels' milk to finish off the meal.

Gamilat, Zara, and I sat down again. "What is our interest in these travelers?" Gamilat asked into the air.

"Sshh," Zara said. She reached over and put a delicate hand over each of our mouths. "They're talking again."

"Where is your wife?" one of them asked Abraham.

"There, in the tent," Abraham said with a wave of his hand.

"I will surely return to you about this time next year, and Sarah your wife will have a son," one of the men said. His voice had a deep intensity and a raw energy I'd never heard before. It soothed like a balm, yet it held heat like the sun.

Abraham nodded his head and smiled. Then the same man stood up and asked. "Why did Sarah laugh just now and say, 'Will I really have a child, now that I am old?'"

Sarah walked meekly out of the tent then. "I did not laugh," she murmured.

"Yes, you did laugh," the man replied. "Is anything too hard for the Lord? I will return to you at the appointed time next year, and you will have a son."

Zara gasped. Her eyes were wide, and her cheeks were flushed. My own heart began to flutter, and I lifted my hands to my chest. I was filled with such inexplicable joy it was almost unbearable. My eyes welled with tears, and I squeezed them shut. When I opened them again, the tears spilled out. Gamilat looked at us.

"What is it?" she asked. "What's wrong? I don't understand." She looked frightened, and I put my hand on her arm.

"See the man in the middle?" She looked and nodded her head.

"He's the Lord!" Zara whispered. Her words were so quiet, they mingled with her breath.

"And the other two?" Gamilat wondered aloud.

"We have only one God," she then declared. "The other two must be God's angels. They're heavenly creatures, divine beings."

Zora looked again. "Oh." Her voice was small

and full of awe. "I've never seen a god that moves and breathes."

Later

Pigat returned a short while later. Her eyes were huge and dark in her pale face. "Those men aren't men," she said. Her chest heaved in and out.

"We already know," Gamilat told her. "Where are they now?"

"Abraham walked with them a short ways," Pigat said. "The two went ahead, and the one—I believe he's the Lord—stayed and talked with Abraham for a little while."

Pigat looked straight into my eyes. "I fear something terrible is about to happen."

My heart lurched. "What makes you say that, Pigat?"

"They talked of the people of Sodom and Gomorrah," she said. "The Lord said their sins are very great. He came down from above to see for himself. Abraham begged him not to destroy the cities if he found ten good men there."

Zara pulled my arm and looked into my face.

"Tell me it isn't true," she cried. "Tell me Lot and his family don't live there." Her eyes were red, and her lips were trembling.

I looked away. "I'm sorry, Zara. I can't tell you what you need to hear. It's true. Lot and his family do live there."

I remembered twenty-three years earlier as if it were yesterday. I was only seven years old then. Abraham and Lot had stood on the edge of a wind-swept cliff on the outskirts of our camp. "I don't want quarreling between you and me," Abraham had said.

Lot had nodded his head.

"The whole land is spread out before you," Abraham had told him. "Let's part company. If you go to the left, I will go to the right. If you go to the right, I will go to the left."

Lot chose the rich, fertile land of the Jordan River Valley.

I remembered Sarah's words when I told her of Lot's choice. "Rhoda," she'd said to me, "Lot lacks wisdom. The land to the east is fertile, yes, but he hasn't considered the people that inhabit that same land. They're a wicked, sinful group of men and women. He'll have to live among them."

It's late, and I can't help thinking on these things. Hori is asleep, but I can't rest. I've tossed and turned until the moon has called to me to get up and write my worries into you, my diary. I've rubbed my pendant between my fingers over and over again. I can no longer trace its outline of the crescent moon. My constant fingering has worn it smooth. For the first time since my mother died twenty-eight years ago, it brings me no comfort. It's cold and lifeless to my touch.

It's Done

Several hours after dawn, Abraham brought this news. He'd left the camp only to return moments later. These were his exact words too. "It's done," he told Sarah. His shoulders were slumped, and there was fear in his eyes. "Great plumes of smoke, like that of a furnace, rise from the east. They come from the direction of the twin cities."

I left the shelter of the tents and walked into the open fields. He was right. Black plumes of furious smoke swelled above the hills. The air was choked with tiny particles of ash now, and I wrapped my scarf around my mouth and nose.

When I returned, pandemonium had struck the camp. "Women and children," Abraham cried, "stay in your tents. Men! Herd the animals farther west!"

I found Zara, Gamilat, and Pigat, and we watched Abraham pace back and forth between the tents. He left suddenly and hiked to the top of a high hill to keep watch. An hour later he ran into the camp. "My nephew returns!" he cried "God has spared his life."

After a short while, Lot staggered into Abraham's arms. His clothes and skin were blackened from the thick smoke. His eyes were bloodshot, and his lips were blistered. Sarah ran toward him. "Are you hurt anywhere?" she asked him.

He shook his head.

"Your wife and daughters, Lot?" she asked. "Where are they?"

"My wife and daughters," he repeated in a hollow voice. "My daughters are in a cave in the mountains. I must return to them. I came only to assure you that I'm not dead."

"Did you leave your wife with them?" Abraham asked.

Lot looked at him. His eyes were blank.

Sarah moved close to Abraham. "There's something wrong," I heard her whisper. "Ask him to tell you the story. Ask him to tell us everything."

Sarah gave Lot a skin of water and helped him to the ground. He gulped the water and poured the rest of it over his head. It ran down his face and streaked his blackened skin.

Abraham sank to the ground beside him. He covered Lot's hand with his own. "Talk to us nephew," Abraham said. "Tell us what happened."

Lot sat for a long moment and said nothing. Then he began to tell the story.

"Last evening," he said, "I sat in the gateway of the city, as usual. The torches were lit, so I could see the path that led to and fro. Two men approached. I remember they were very tall, and their shoulders were unusually broad."

Gamilat inhaled sharply and looked at me.

"I rose to greet them," Lot said, "and I knew at once that the men were angels." He glanced at Abraham beside him. "Uncle, I don't know how I knew this. I've never seen an angel before, but somehow I just knew."

I saw Abraham squeeze his hand.

Lot continued, "I bowed at once and put my face in the dirt. 'Please turn aside to your servant's house,' I told them. 'You can wash your feet and spend the night. Then you can go on your way early in the morning.'

"I led them through the city to my house. The people were still in the streets, making merry with wine. They followed the angels with their eyes. We arrived, and I prepared a meal. After we ate, as we readied our beds for slumber, there was a great commotion outside the house."

Lot paused. He put his head in his hands to compose himself.

"What happened?" Abraham asked.

"I opened the door, and . . ." He paused and looked into Abraham's eyes. "I've never seen anything like it. Hundreds of men surrounded the house. Some were very old, and some were just boys." His voice broke. "Children, in fact. I shut the door behind me, and they shouted, 'Where are the men who came with you? Bring them out!'"

Sarah shuddered and put her hand to her mouth. The wind had shifted to the west, and the ash drifted lazily over the camp. We were dusted in gray flakes, and the sun was veiled in the smoky sky. Lot chocked back sobs.

"What then, nephew?" Abraham urged. "Tell us what happened next."

"They were pushing past me and trying to break down the door, when I felt it give without warning behind me. I was pulled in by the hands of the angels. The door was shut and bolted tight. Then I heard screams outside. The men shouted that they were blind. They stumbled about and couldn't find the door.

"The first rays of dawn shone through my window, and all at once the angels cried, 'Hurry! Take your wife and your two daughters and leave the city at once. The outcry of the Lord against its people is too great. The Lord has sent us to destroy this place.'"

Lot's eyes were filled with horror. "I froze," he said. "I couldn't move. I had the distant sensation that someone was leading me away from my house. We were outside, and I realized the angels had pulled us all out.

"'Flee for your lives!' they cried to us. 'Don't

look back and don't stop anywhere in the plain! Flee to the mountains, or you will be swept away.'"

Lot put his head in Abraham's lap then and began to sob. His wails filled the camp.

"My wife!" he cried. "She didn't listen. We smelled the sulfur in the air, and we heard the screams of the people. I held her hand and ran with her. My children were on my other side. Then there was a sudden explosion. She let go of my hand, and I lost her.

"It wasn't until later, when we stood on a crest of a mountain, that I knew it was safe to look back. There was nothing left of the cities but two smoking mounds of ashes. On my way here, I ran to the spot where I lost her. I thought I might find my wife, injured or ill in the dirt. There was nothing left but a pillar of salt."

He looked at Sarah now. "I know you'll think me strange to say this, but I recognized my wife in that pillar of salt." He pointed toward the east. "She's still there, frozen in salt for her disobedience."

Lot Has Left for the Mountains

His daughters wait for him there. Hori called our own children to our tent. He put a hand on both Neri and Zara and said we should sit on piles of blankets. We waited for Hori to speak to us.

"What will Papa teach us today?" Neri whispered to me with a twinkle in his eyes. He's a younger version of Hori, and he knows it. Sometimes he imitates his father's mannerisms just to irritate him. He sat cross-legged and stroked his cheek with his finger while he watched his father do the same.

Whenever Hori glanced his way, Neri would stop. This would normally send Zara into a fit of laughter. Today, Zara, the sensitive one, sensed her father's pensive mood and gave Neri a cross look.

"There's an important lesson I want you to take away from Lot's experience," Hori told them. He looked at me. "Rhoda, even you will benefit from these words."

Neri heard the urgency in his father's voice and sat up.

"There are three things to remember," Hori said. "When the angels said, 'Don't look back,' they told Lot not to return to sin. To look back toward the twin cities was to look back toward a world of sin.

"Next," Hori continued, "they said, 'Don't stop anywhere in the plain.'"

"Yes, Papa," Zara interrupted. "He told Lot and his family not to stay where they already were. They were comfortable there, and they knew the road well. He wanted them to go to a different place now."

Hori grinned with pride at Zara. "That's right. Last, the angel said, 'Flee to the mountains!'"

With these words, my husband looked into my eyes. Zara and Neri looked at me as well. My cheeks were flushed, and the metal charm I'd worn for so many years burned on my throat.

Neri said softly, "Reach toward God. He wanted them to leave their old world behind, run toward God, and trust him for protection and refuge."

I looked at my children. I was amazed at their wisdom. Hori had taught them well. How I wish their grandfather could hear them. He would've been so proud of their faith and their devotion to the one true God he loved.

"Has the day come so soon that I must take instruction from my children?" I asked them with a laugh. "Have you become my sages at such an early age?"

My heart thumped in my chest. How could I expect my children to put their faith and trust in God if I didn't? My hands shook as I reached up to untie the leather string.

I didn't even know if I could do it.

Neri jumped up to help me. "Let me do it for you, Mama," he said. Zara came around, and she held up my hair. I felt Neri's rough fingers on my neck, and then the charm fell into my lap.

They watched me as I stared at it without moving. The last time I'd seen it anywhere except around my neck was when Papa gave it to me. I was three years old. I'd loosened the string since then, but I'd never let it leave my neck. Not once in all these years.

I was reminded of Mama, and my throat became tight. It used to reflect the sunlight when she walked outside. I don't ever remember her not wearing it. I inhaled deeply and touched my bare throat. I felt naked and vulnerable.

I thought back to when I first left Haran with Abram and Sarai. I rode away on Naamah, and I turned my head to see my home before it faded away. Sarai saw me and said, 'Look ahead, Rhoda. Never look behind."

Don't look back . . . I realized now that I had looked behind all of my life. I was no different than Lot's wife. It could just as easily have been me on the plain of the Jordan, embedded in a pillar of salt.

Don't stop anywhere in the plain . . . I hadn't just stopped on the plain—I was stuck there. It was time for me to leave. Time for me to flee to the mountains! I knew now where I had to go.

I held the charm in my hand and brought it to my lips. "This isn't a good-bye, Mama," I told myself. "It's like Javen said. You swim in my veins. You'll always be with me. I have to let go of idols. That's what this charm is. It doesn't protect me. God does. I have to run to God now. He is my mountain. I have to trust him."

The tears began to flow, and I felt a release. Zara, Neri, and Hori wrapped their arms around me. I'd never need a charm to know I was blessed.

Another Sadness

We've moved our tents southwest to the Valley of Gerar and are deep in the Negev Desert again, but our camp isn't far from the coast. The land is rich and well watered. There's a salty breeze that blows in from the Great Sea. Still, there are no more hills splashed with grapes. And I'm not happy.

This morning, officials came and took Sarah to the palace of Gerar. I can't believe it's happened again. I didn't even know until Zara came to find me. I felt weak in my knees.

"How do you know?" I asked her. "Why was she taken?"

"Pigat told me. She was there when it happened," Zara said through her tears.

"Abraham told them she was his sister, so King Abimelech sent for her."

I sank to the ground. I'm not there for her this time. What will she do? Zara sits next to me as I write out my sadness, but even her presence doesn't comfort me.

Oh, Happy Day!

Each morning at daybreak, I've stood at the edge of camp and surveyed the horizon for a sign of Sarah's return. I've done the same during the cool of the day. Then a flock of quail fluttered across the trade route today! I saw a bevy of sheep and oxen emerge from the haze. Male and female slaves sauntered beside them. In front was an official. And Sarah rode beside him on a donkey!

I ran to greet her.

She flew from the donkey's back and embraced me. "I was lost without you this time," she said. She bent toward my ear. "Don't concern yourself. God protected me, and nothing happened. The only harm I felt was that I was just alone and homesick."

We walked hand and hand, and Abraham met us before we reached the camp. His eyes were sunken. He'd been so withdrawn since Sarah was taken.

"King Abimelech wishes you to know that his land is before you. You may live wherever you like," the official said curtly. He turned to Sarah. "It is the king's desire for your husband to accept one thousand shekels of silver. This is to cover the offense against you before all who are with you; you are completely vindicated."

The official turned and went on his way, leaving behind a pouch of silver, the cattle, and the servants.

"What does this mean?" I asked Sarah.

"The King didn't know I was married," she told me. "God appeared to him in a dream and told him so. The silver, the cattle, and the servants are his payment to Abraham for taking a married woman into his household. It's his attempt to rectify the wrong he committed."

Abraham retreated for a time to pray for King Abimelech and his household.

When he returned, Abraham insisted that a lamb be slaughtered to celebrate Sarah's return. We prepared a feast. The grain was ground, and we made bread and porridge sweetened with honey. The lamb was wrapped in grape leaves and roasted over the fire. There was also a soup thick with peas, beans, and lentils, and dried figs boiled in grape molasses.

One of the servants brought out a lyre and another a lute. The twang of their strings ushered in the violet twilight. As the darkness descended on the camp, each of the families retreated into their tents, happy that our household was complete again. I'm glad to have happy things to record after so much sadness lately.

God is good.

It's a Miracle!

I was in the grove gathering wood when I heard footsteps in the dried leaves. Pigat was out of breath. "Drop the sticks," she cried. "Come now."

The sticks fell to the ground, and I stood up straight. The hair on my arms was on end. "What is it?" I asked her. "Has something happened?"

"Just come," Gamilat urged.

They pulled me to Sarah's tent, and when I pushed aside the flap, Sarah rushed to me and held my hands. "I'm with child," she said. Her eyes were like brilliant jewels, and her cheeks were flushed.

I opened my mouth, but the words wouldn't come. I was overwhelmed with emotions. Nearly twenty-five years ago God had promised Sarah a child, and now, at last, the promise is nearly delivered. But Sarah is eighty-nine years old!

It's a marvel. All these years my heart has ached

for her. Now at last she will experience the joy and fulfillment of motherhood that even I have known.

Later

I can't help but want to be around Sarah every minute now. After she told us the news and we each went our own ways for a bit, I came back to her and put my arms around her and I held her close to me. She's like my mother. My love for her is so deep it can't be measured.

I pulled away and looked into her eyes. "God made your womb fruitful, Sarah. It's no longer barren. God is doing what he said he'd do. He's faithful to keep his promise."

Sarah fell to her knees and began to weep. Her shoulders shook, and her chest heaved until wrenching sobs tore free. Pigat came in then and held her face in her hands, and Gamilat clung to her for support.

When Sarah lifted her face, the tears poured from her eyes. "The thing I've feared the most hasn't come to pass," she cried. "Abraham's seed will live in our child. My womb will bear him a son. God hasn't forsaken his servant Sarah."

She lay on the floor for a long time, spent with joy

and relief and gratitude. She loved her husband beyond measure, but I knew she believed that their union was finally complete on this day.

A New Love

As Sarah's belly grows rounder, she sings like a songbird. I never knew she had such a sweet voice. She was filled with laughter before, but her joy has increased tenfold. Abraham seems changed as well, and I'm reminded that the promise God made wasn't just for Sarah but also for him.

He's one hundred years old now, and he's spry. There's a bounce in his step that I never noticed before. When he passes his wife, he rubs his hand over her bulging belly with such love.

Hori explained this to me one day. "It's one thing to love a woman," he said, "but that love can reach an even higher plateau when your child is in her womb. It bonds a man to a woman so deeply that nothing can break that tie. Not separation and not even death."

He held me close. "Abraham loves Sarah in a new way, but I've had the joy of loving you this way ever since I can remember."

The Night Seems Long

I was awakened by a noise I thought I recognized. I sat up and listened. I heard Hori's soft snores and the steady, rhythmic chirp of the crickets, but I knew there was something else. I walked to the door and quieted my breath. Then I lifted up the tent flap and tuned my ear to the sounds in the camp.

There was a groan. Zara walked toward me sleepily, and Hori, just awakened, stood behind me. He rested his hand on my shoulder.

I walked toward Pigat's tent and arrived just as she walked out with Jairus. I heard it again. It came from Sarah's tent. Pigat went inside, and I left to awaken Gamilat. We knew what it was.

When I returned, Pigat stuck her head out of Sarah's tent and nodded. "It's time," she said.

Gamilat ran toward me. "Where's Javen?" I asked her.

"He went to awaken Dibri and Lois," she said. "Is there anything we can do?"

"Pigat will tell us," I said.

At that moment Abraham carried Sarah in his arms to the birth tent. Her belly was enormous, and her face was crumpled in pain. Pigat followed close behind.

Javen arrived with Dibri and Lois. I touched my older brother's pale face. "Still troubled about this after all these years?" I asked. Javen nodded.

Abraham walked out. His face was drained of color, and he stood near the tent helplessly. Every time he heard Sarah cry, he jumped and wrung his hands together. Javen put his arm around his shoulders and led him to a blanket spread on the ground. They looked like frightened children, and I couldn't help but smile.

We're all waiting.

The Baby Has Come!

After some time, Gamilat had gathered several bowls of water and lit more lamps. I soaked a cloth in water and rubbed the perspiration from Sarah's forehead. All at once, her face contorted in pain, and she cried out. Before any of us knew what had happened, she had pushed her baby from her womb.

Pigat was so startled! She stared at the baby and then at Sarah with wide eyes.

His head was covered in a thick mop of hair!

Pigat worked quickly on the baby until he cried—his lungs were working! Pigat placed the baby on Sarah's chest. Sarah smiled with such wonder as she wrapped her arms around her son's tiny body.

She looked at me with a smile, and then all at once she began to laugh. It was a glorious, rolling laughter that brought tears to my eyes. Abraham entered the tent and walked over to his wife and son. He couldn't speak, and he rubbed his eyes with his hand. Then he began to laugh as well.

Salty tears rolled into my mouth, and I laughed, then cried, then laughed some more. We all knew as we looked at the baby that we'd witnessed a miracle. A ninety-year-old woman had just given her one-hundred-year-old husband the child of their heart. And God had already established a covenant with this baby!

I flashed back to my little home in Haran when Javen had sat across the table from me. "Rhoda," Javen had said, Abraham is a follower of the one true God. Abraham has even heard God's voice. This God promised to make him into a great nation. He promised to bless him. Someday Abraham's name will be great and he will be known everywhere!

I looked at Abraham and Sarah, and little Isaac cradled in his mother's arms. God had fulfilled his promise. I touched my bare neck and smiled. This God is the only true God. I'd finally let go of my fear and learned to trust him. Sarah had too. She would never doubt God again.

She reached for Abraham's hand. "God has brought me laughter, and everyone who hears about this will laugh with me. Who would have said to Abraham that Sarah would nurse children? Yet I have borne him a son in his old age."

Abraham put his forehead against Sarah's and rested there.

I walked outside and fell into Hori's arms. There was a crescent moon in the sky, and it reminded me of Mama. It always would.

"It is said," he whispered into my ear, "that with the birth of each child, a wave passes through the universe. If you gaze into the sky at the exact moment, you can see the heavens ripple."

I believe that.

EPILOGUE

One year after Isaac was born, Gamilat found her womb full again. Her body, worn from her previous pregnancies, could not withstand another birth. She died while giving life to her last child, a girl.

Javen was heartbroken. He named his daughter Zebudah in honor of his mother, who had also died while giving life.

Dibri, Javen, and Rhoda remained close through the years. Though Pigat and Rhoda were devastated by the loss of their friend Gamilat, they devoted themselves to helping Javen raise his new daughter.

Sarah and Abraham held a great feast to honor their son Isaac about two years after his birth. Ishmael, resentful of Isaac's elevated status in the household, openly mocked his half-brother. Sarah was outraged. She demanded that Hagar and Ishmael be sent away. Mother and son wandered in the desert of Beersheba under God's watchful eye. Eventually, Ishmael settled in the Desert of Paran and became an archer. Hagar traveled to her homeland of Egypt to find a wife for her son. Today, Ishmael is considered the father of the Arab nation.

Several years passed, and God called Abraham to sacrifice Isaac upon Mount Moriah. It would prove to be the greatest test of Abraham's faith. Isaac was bound upon the altar, and in agony Abraham held a knife above his son. God was satisfied with Abraham's obedience. He told him not to lay a hand on the boy.

Then God renewed his promise with Abraham. He promised to bless him and make his descendants as numerous as the stars in the sky and the sand on the seashore.

Sarah lived long enough to raise the son of her dreams. At 127 years old, she closed her eyes for the last time. She died in Hebron, in the land of Canaan, where she had lived many years. Abraham purchased the field of Machpelah, and lovingly buried her in a cave there near the oaks of Mamre where God had appeared to him.

All of the members of Abraham's household mourned the passing of their beloved mistress. Zara, Julia, and Phoebe lived in other households at the time of Sarah's death. They returned to Hebron with their husbands and married children for Sarah's burial. They wished to pay their respects and give homage to the extraordinary matriarch who had shaped all of their lives.

Pigat was seventy-five at the time of Sarah's death. Her devotion to her mistress proved to be her downfall. She was grief-stricken, and she died within the year.

Abraham found a wife for his son in his homeland of Mesopotamia. Isaac and Rebekah were married in Sarah's tent. Though his mother was not alive, her presence surrounded Isaac and brought him great comfort.

Later Abraham took another wife by the name of Keturah. She bore him six sons: Zimran, Jokshan, Medan, Midian, Ishbak, and Shuah. He lived to be 175 years old. Both Isaac and Ishmael buried him with his beloved wife Sarah in the cave in the field of Machpelah. Today Abraham is considered the father of the Hebrew nation.

Rhoda and Hori lived to an old age, though they died well before Abraham. When Rhoda passed away first, Javen and Dibri requested Hori's permission to bury her in Haran close to her mother and father. Hori agreed. All of her loved ones, including Zara and Neri and their children, gathered close to the cave. They tore their clothes in grief as they murmured their farewells.

Three years later, Hori was buried beside her. Their marriage union had endured for sixty joyous years.

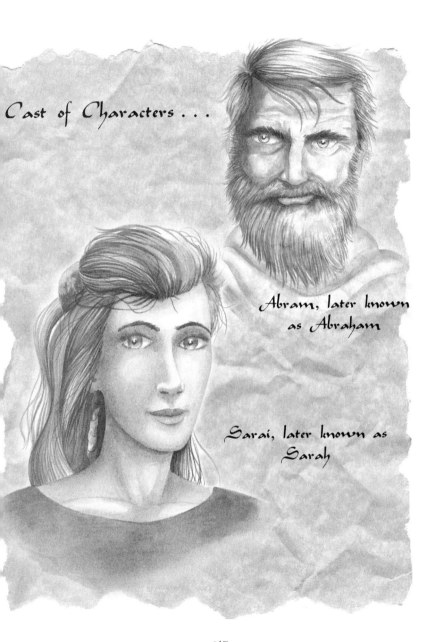

Cast of Characters . . .

Abram, later known as Abraham

Sarai, later known as Sarah

The Route

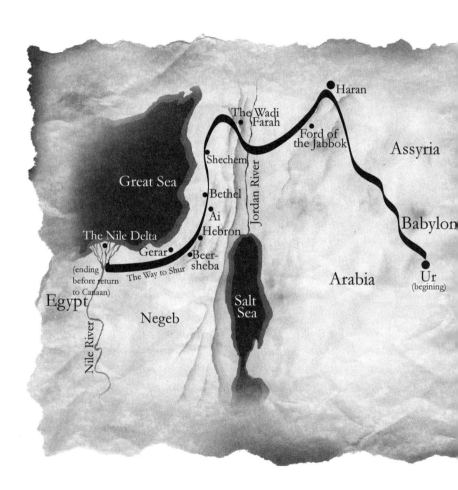

Haran

The Wadi Farah

Ford of the Jabbok

Assyria

Shechem

Jordan River

Great Sea

Bethel

Ai

Babylon

Hebron

The Nile Delta

Gerar

Beer-sheba

Ur
(begining)

(ending
before return
to Canaan)

The Way to Shur

Egypt

Arabia

Salt
Sea

Nile River

Negeb

RHODA'S JOURNEY

Rhoda's story begins in the city of Haran in northern Mesopotamia, between the Tigris and Euphrates Rivers. Then Rhoda's journey takes her to the land of Canaan, across the great Negev Desert, and into Egypt. Her travels are set approximately between the years 2091 B.C. to 2066 B.C.

The People Rhoda Wrote of Most

Abram:	The father of the Israelites, given his new name *Abraham* when God made a covenant with him
Sarai:	The wife of Abram, given her new name *Sarah* when God made a covenant with her husband
Herself:	Sarah's traveling companion *
Javen:	Rhoda's older brother *
Dibri:	Rhoda's younger brother *
Mama:	Rhoda's mother *
Papa:	Rhoda's father *
Gamilat:	A servant to Sarah and friend to Rhoda *
Pigat:	Also a servant to Sarah and friend to Rhoda *

The People Rhoda Encountered

(in order of appearance)

Terah: Abraham's father

Lot: Abraham's nephew

Bedouins: Desert nomads

Hori: Rhoda's husband *

Hagar: Sarah's Egyptian maidservant and mother to Ishmael

Ishmael: The son of Abraham and Hagar

Zara: The daughter of Rhoda and Hori *

Neri: The son of Rhoda and Hori *

Isaac: The long-awaited, promised son of Abraham and Sarah. His name means laughter.

denotes fictional characters

The Patriarchs

Abraham's Family Tree
(Book of Genesis)

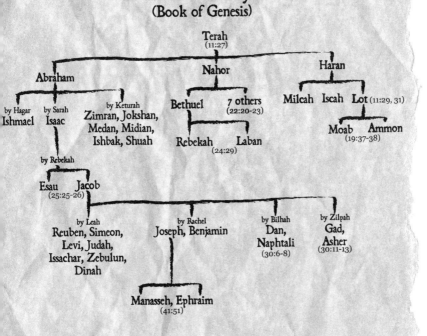

Terah
(11:27)

Abraham   Nahor   Haran

by Hagar   by Sarah   by Keturah
Ishmael   Isaac   Zimran, Jokshan,   Bethuel   7 others   Milcah   Iscah   Lot (11:29, 31)
            Medan, Midian,   (22:20-23)
            Ishbak, Shuah   Rebekah   Laban   Moab   Ammon
                                            (24:29)   (19:37-38)

by Rebekah
Esau   Jacob
(25:25-26)

by Leah   by Rachel   by Bilhah   by Zilpah
Reuben, Simeon,   Joseph, Benjamin   Dan,   Gad,
Levi, Judah,   Naphtali   Asher
Issachar, Zebulun,   (30:6-8)   (30:11-13)
Dinah

Manasseh, Ephraim
(41:51)

TRACING HISTORY: A TIMELINE

2296 B.C.

Terah is born. He lives in the city of Ur of the Chaldeens, where he raises three sons.

2166 B.C.

Abram is born when his father Terah is 130 years old. His brothers are Nahor and Haran.

2156 B.C.

Sarai is born.

2156–2091 B.C.

Abram and Sarai marry. God tells Abram to leave Ur of the Chaldeens and "go to a land I will show you." They journey north to Haran with Terah and Lot, whose father, Haran, has died. Terah chooses to settle in Haran even though Abram knows they should continue on to the land of Canaan.

2091 B.C.

Terah dies in Haran at 205 years of age. Abram and Sarai leave and continue their long-awaited journey to the land of Canaan with Lot in tow.

2091–2080 B.C.

Abram and his household travel farther south to Egypt when a famine threatens Canaan. Here Abram passes Sarai off as his sister, and she is taken into Pharaoh's palace for a time. She is allowed to leave when God sends plagues upon the king's household.

Abram is rich in cattle and servants, presents from Pharaoh, when he returns to Canaan. He eventually parts company with Lot. His nephew settles in the east, and Abram settles in the west.

2080 B.C.

God promises to give Sarai a son, but she loses faith and takes matters into her own hands. Sarai gives Abram her Egyptian maidservant, Hagar. Hagar becomes Abram's second wife and gives birth to his first child, Ishmael.

2067 B.C.

God confirms his covenant with Abram and Sarai and changes their names to Abraham and Sarah. All males over the age of eight days are circumcised as an everlasting sign of this covenant.

God promises to give Sarah a son called Isaac and establish his covenant with him. He promises to bless Ishmael as well.

The Lord and two angels visit Abraham's camp. The Lord reminds Sarah that in a year's time she will give birth to her son.

The angels proceed to Sodom and Gomorrah, and the city is destroyed not long after. Only Lot and his two daughters are spared.

Abraham moves his household to Gerar in the region of the Negev. Once again, Abraham passes Sarah off as his sister. She is coveted by King Abimelech and taken into his harem for a time. God protects her, and she is returned unharmed.

Sarah gives birth to Isaac, just as God promised. She is ninety-years old, and Abraham is one hundred years old.

2064 B.C.

Isaac is weaned, and a great celebration is held. When Ishmael, now sixteen years of age, mocks Isaac, Sarah tells Abraham to send him and his mother away.

2029 B.C.

Sarah dies at the age of 127 years. Isaac is 36 years old at the time. Abraham purchases the field of Machpelah from Ephron the Hittite for four hundred shekels of silver. He buries Sarah in a cave.

2026 B.C.

Isaac marries Rebekah.

1991 B.C.

Abraham dies. He is 175 years old. Isaac and Ishmael reunite to bury their father with Sarah in the cave of Machpelah.

* all dates prior to 1886 B.C. are historically uncertain.

The Landscape . . .

Acacia trees like this dot the landscape of the Negev. Desert nomads, like the Bedouins, consider them holy.

The Olive Tree is the most sacred of all the trees mentioned in the Bible. It has a low, knotty trunk and can live for more than one thousand years.

Arabian camel

...ven said camels were
...tter suited for long
...eks. It was a burden for
...aamah to carry heavy
...ads in the desert.

Naamah

A section of an
Egyptian sanatoria

The sanatoria, similar to a
complex of hospitals, was
located near the temple.
The sick or injured came
here when they wanted to
get well.

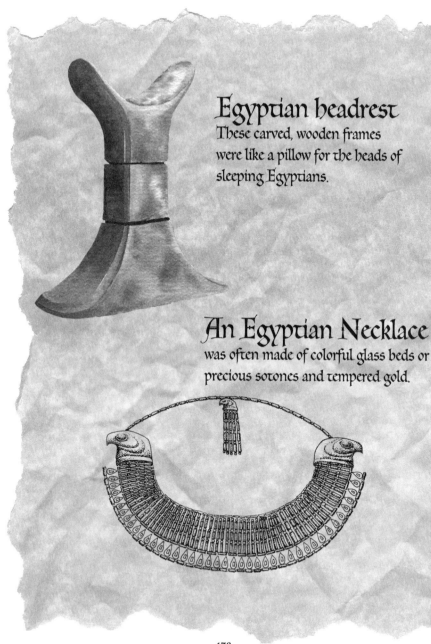

Egyptian headrest

These carved, wooden frames were like a pillow for the heads of sleeping Egyptians.

An Egyptian Necklace

was often made of colorful glass beds or precious sotones and tempered gold.

CAANAN'S PLACE IN HISTORY

When God told Abram, "Leave your country, your people and your father's household and go to the land I will show you," he was referring to the land called Canaan. When Abram arrived, God revealed his plan and told him, "To your offspring I will give this land."

Canaan is one of the oldest names for Palestine, and today it is known as Israel. The Canaanites lived in walled cities, many of them along the Great Sea (now called the Mediterranean Sea) on the western coast. The rulers of the cities constantly fought with one another, and they lived under continual threat of attack from their own neighbors. They worshiped many gods, which they viewed as having characteristics similar to humans.

Huge temples were built to worship these and other gods. The kings of the Canaanite cities took great pride in building temples as grand and glorious as possible. The statues of the gods and the walls of the shrines were covered in gold. Golden bowls with special food were placed at the foot of the statues to feed the gods.

The most important contribution of the Canaanites to the world was found deep in the turquoise mines in the heart of the Sinai desert. Inscriptions by the Canaanite miners revealed the very first alphabet! It is believed to have been invented between 2000 and 1600 B.C. All alphabets since then were derived from this first ancient alphabet of the Canaanites, comprised of twenty-two letters.

THEN AND NOW

The City of Hebron

Meaning "friend of God" in Arabic, Hebron is an ancient city—maybe as old as the beginning of the world, since tradition says it was once home to Adam.

Located nineteen miles southwest of Jerusalem, the city of Hebron was on the main road to Beersheba. The hills surrounding the city grew fine grapes, and Hebron was known for the excellent wine it produced.

King David ruled from Hebron for seven years before moving the capital to Jerusalem when he became king of both Israel and Judah, about 993 B.C.

Today Hebron is located in the West Bank. Although it was incorporated into Jordan in 1948, it was seized by Israel during the Six-Day War in 1967. A few hundred Jewish Israelis settled into central Hebron amidst tens of thousands of Palestinians, and the tension between the two groups has not abated.

The Cave of Machpelah, also known as the Tomb of the Patriarchs, contains the burial sites of Abraham and Sarah, Isaac and Rebekah, and Jacob and Leah. It is the second most holy site in Judaism, next to the Temple Mount in Jerusalem. A synagogue and mosque were built over the tomb. In 1862 the prince of Wales was the first European permitted to enter the holy mosque.

In the Valley of Eshcol, about three miles north of Hebron, stands one of the largest oak trees in Israel. It is believed by some to be the ancient tree under which Abraham pitched his tent. It has been named "Abraham's Oak."

The Cities of Sodom and Gomorrah

As two of the five "Cities of the Plain," Sodom and Gomorrah were located somewhere around the area of the Salt Sea (now called the Dead Sea). These two Cities of the Plain, along with the other three— Admah, Zeboiim, and Zoar—were surrounded by the lush, watered land of the Jordanian Plain. It was here that Lot parted company with Abraham and chose this attractive country for his home, leaving his uncle the less fertile land of Canaan. After the cities were destroyed, the land became barren.

Though Sodom and Gomorrah are classified as "lost," it's widely believed that their remains lie beneath the Dead Sea. Whether it is the northern end or the southern end is still disputed.

The Dead Sea was known in ancient times as the Salt Sea. It is really a lake and lies between the countries of Israel and Jordan. It is known to the Arabs as *Bahr Lot*, which means the "Sea of Lot."

With an elevation of thirteen hundred feet below sea level, it is the lowest point on earth. It is seven times as salty as the ocean, enabling greater buoyancy. Its high concentration of other minerals such as calcium, potassium, magnesium, and bromide make the water very therapeutic but bitter to the taste and oily to the touch.

Signs are posted along many of the beaches in Hebrew, Aramaic, and English, warning the bathers not to drink the water and not to splash on other swimmers.

The Dead Sea is fed daily by the Jordan River with no less than six million tons of water.

Though the lake has no outlet, its level is maintained by pure evaporation, sometimes so intense that a thick blue haze is formed over the surface of the lake. Chunks of pure salt as large as automobiles are formed after the water has evaporated. While the Dead Sea cannot sustain any life—fish released into the water from the Jordan River die almostimmediately—an abundance of wildlife lives on its banks, feeding on the dead fish that wash ashore.

BIBLIOGRAPHY

Many sources were consulted and used in research for writing Rhoda's and Sarah's story in the Promised Land Diaries series, including:

Adam Clarke's Commentary on the Bible, Adam Clarke, abridged by Ralph H. Earle (World Bible Publishing Co., 1996).

Atlas of the Bible: An Illustrated Guide to the Holy Land, edited by Joseph L. Gardner (The Readers Digest Association, 1981).

The Biblical Times, edited by Derek Williams (Baker Books, a division of Baker Book House Co., 1997).

Jamieson, Fausset, and Brown's Commentary on the Whole Bible, Fausset, Brown, Robert Jamieson (Zondervan Publishing House, 1999).

Matthew Henry's Commentary on the Whole Bible: Complete and Unabridged in One Volume, Matthew Henry (Hendrickson Publishers, 1991).

Meredith's Book of Bible Lists, J. L. Meredith (Bethany House Publishers, 1980).

Nelson's Illustrated Encyclopedia of the Bible, edited by John Drane (Thomas Nelson, Inc., 2001).

The New International Dictionary of the Bible, revising editor J. D. Douglas, general editor Merrill C. Tenney (Zondervan Publishing House, 1987).

The Picture Bible Dictionary, Berkeley and Alvera Mickelsen (Chariot Books, an imprint of David C. Cook Publishing Co., 1993).

Women of the Bible: A One-Year Devotional Study of Women in Scripture, Ann Spangler and Jean Syswerda (Zondervan, 1999).

ABOUT THE AUTHOR

Anne Tyra Adams is the author of eight children's books, several of which have been translated into three foreign languages: Indonesian, Korean, and Afrikaans. Two of her books, *The New Kids Book of Bible Facts* and *The Baker Book of Bible Travels for Kids,* provided the foundation for writing this series, the Promised Land Diaries.

A journalist and detailed researcher, Adams is also a "student of ancient history," with a deep fascination for the Jewish culture. She used all this experience, love of history, and curiosity to write this book.

When not working on more Promised Land Diaries, Adams loves to read the classics and ancient history, taking many armchair travels in time to foreign lands. She especially loves reading biographies of famous authors.

She and her husband and their two children live in Phoenix, Arizona. They often hike in the mountainous desert surrounding their home and have been known to spot quail, coyote, an occasional fox, and many lizards. Not to be outdone by the great outdoors, they share their home with three dogs, a cat, and an assortment of little fish.

ABOUT THE ILLUSTRATOR

Dennis Edwards is the illustrator of three big Bible story-books: *Heroes of the Bible, Boys Life Adventures,* and *My Bible Journey.* As a designer and illustrator he's also contributed to numerous others.

His favorite books include Robert Louis Stevenson's *Treasure Island,* comic books, and science fiction-related books because "the sky's the limit!"

Dennis also enjoys acting, and sometimes gets to perform for the kids at his church.

Books in

Series
1
Persia's Brightest Star
The Diary of Queen Esther's Attendant

2
The Laughing Princess of the Desert
The Diary of Sarah's Traveling Companion

Coming in Spring 2004:

3
Priceless Jewel at the Well
The Diary of Rebekah's Nursemaid

4
The Peaceful Warrior
The Diary of Deborah's Armor Bearer

For Michal Tyra and Alexandra Tyra, whose potential knows no boundaries.

The author would like to thank everyone at Educational Publishing Concepts, the talented Dennis Edwards, the team at Baker Book House Company, and Tina Novinski.

Copyright © 2003 by Baker Book House

Published by Baker Books
a division of Baker Book House Company
P.O. Box 6287, Grand Rapids, MI 49516-6287
www.bakerbooks.com

Printed in the United States of America

Library of Congress Cataloging-in-Publication Data on file.

ISBN 0-8010-4523-1

Scripture is taken from the HOLY BIBLE, NEW INTERNATIONAL VERSION®. NIV®. Copyright © 1973, 1978, 1984 by International Bible Society. Used by permission of Zondervan. All rights reserved.

Series Creator: Jerry Watkins and Educational Publishing Concepts, with Anne Tyra Adams
Designer and Illustrator: Dennis Edwards
Editors: Jeanette Thomason, Kelley Meyne

The biblical account of Sarah can be found in the Bible's Old Testament, Genesis 11–27. While Rhoda's dairies and the epilogue are based on this and historical accounts, the character of Rhoda, her diaries, and some of the minor events described are works of fiction.